KNOTS

A Novel

Stanley Cutler

Published by the Author
PHILADELPHIA, PENNSYLVANIA

§

To Betsy

§

Know that enough is enough,
and you'll always have enough.

"Tao Te Ching of Lao Tsu", verse 46
Translated by B. B. Walker

PART ONE

The End of the Road

After sundown, after the dishes have been stowed away and they are getting Hannah ready for bed, a small man wearing a cowboy hat knocks on the aluminum screen door of their travel trailer. The fellow wears a faded canvas jacket over a soiled plaid shirt. His pants are caked with barnyard dust and have deep creases behind the knees. He smells of manure. A horse, vague in the darkness beyond the illumination of the trailer's interior lights, stands loosely tethered to a mesquite bush.

The trailer the Bermans live in is a box with seats that convert to beds, a mini-kitchen, and a panel door that conceals a toilet and a sink. For the past few months, when they have not been together inside the trailer, the Bermans have been inside their car traveling to the next campsite. Now, on a November evening in 1973, the car and trailer are parked on beaten earth behind an enormous sand dune that rises several feet above the trailer roof. The dune faces the Sea of Cortez on the West coast of Mexico.

1

The man in the cowboy hat has bad news for them – they can't camp here. "*Aqui campimento es no permisso*," he says.

Michael does not want to hitch up and journey back to the main highway on a twisting dirt road after dark. Then where would they go? The daylong drive through the Sonora Desert had been made slowly, without air conditioning, requiring vigilant attention to the dashboard thermometer. Four-year old Hannah had been red-eyed and cranky by the time they finally got here. His wife, Karen, who had endured the ride in tight-lipped anticipation of an imminent breakdown, is in no mood for eviction.

Michael knows some Spanish vocabulary and remembers a few conversational phrases from his school days. Perhaps he'll be able to negotiate a deal, perhaps the fellow will take money and allow them to spend the night. "Quien usted?" he asks.

"*Yo soy el guardián rancho. Campimento es no permisso.*"

"Por que no?"

"*Por que es la regla, y yo soy el guardián de la finca.*" Because it's the rule, and he is watchman of the estate.

Michael opens the door, steps outside, and invites the man to enter with a welcoming sweep of his arm.

"*No. No me,*" says the guy, waving his hands down his front, gesturing at his clothes. "*Yo soy muy sucia.*" True enough, he's dirty.

"Would you like *una cerveza*?" Michael pops the cap of an imaginary beer bottle. He is certain of the word for beer because of the billboards.

The man looks toward Hannah and Karen standing in the doorway and touches the brim of his once-white hat. "*Buenas*," he says politely.

"Una cerveza?"

"*Si, si*," says the watchman, smiling, showing a gap where he's lost a front tooth.

Good, the man is willing to negotiate. Now the challenge will be to arrange a deal in a language he barely understands. He gets the bottles from the little refrigerator and carries them outside. He sits on the ground and gestures to a spot nearby, suggesting that the fellow ought to join him on the dirt so that they might discuss the matter at hand as equals. The man shrugs and folds to the ground.

"Mi nombre es Michael... Miguel. Y usted?"

"*Mi nombre es Fernando,*"

Michael offers his hand. Fernando takes it, "*Mucho gusto... Miguel,*" he says.

"Mucho gusto, Fernando," Michael responds.

He inquires about the horse, remembering the word '*caballo*.' Fernando says it is the horse he prefers, a good horse, though quite small as horses go.

Little Hannah leaves the confinement of the trailer and approaches the tired, head-low nag. This is as close as she has ever been to a horse and she is fascinated. Karen comes to sit by Michael's side, wrapping the long skirt around her shins.

Fernando says that yes, he lives at the ranchero called *Los Algodones*, also called *Catch Veintidos*, pronouncing 'Catch' in a Spanish way, as '*Kati-jé.*' He accepts a cigarette, makes himself comfortable, extends his legs, crossing them at the ankles. They agree that the beach and the sea and the mountains are beautiful at the ranch called *Los Algodones*, named after a few cottonwood trees struggling against the onslaughts of mesquite and cactus on the narrow plain between the sea and rugged hills.

The Bermans had not known about this place when they'd crossed the border at Tijuana two days ago. They'd learned about it from a French hippie at a campground a hundred miles South of the border. The Frenchman told them of a special, wild place, only a day's drive farther South, where the movie of *Catch-22* had been filmed, and where there were good campsites by the sea. He had drawn them a map, warning that there were no road signs pointing to Catch-22 from the highway, that the place was hard to find, but well worth the effort.

Three years before, in 1970, a movie company had fabricated an imitation of a World War Two airfield by putting down an asphalt airstrip and building sets imitating bomb-damaged Italian houses. Driving past the sets on the way in from the highway, the structures had seemed to Michael to be the way they had looked in the movie. If he can persuade Fernando to let them stay, he would examine them tomorrow.

As Fernando drains the bottle, Michael asks, "Mañana? Es mañana okay?"

"*Si. Mañana es okay*," answers the ranch hand, reasonably, as if to say that he is not the sort to displace a nice family at night.

The trailer interior is almost a cube. In the back, under a wide window, is a bench sofa. In the front, there is a drop-down table flanked by dining benches. At night, they lower the table, open the bench cushions, and form their bed. Hannah sleeps above them, on cushions laid across a pull-down shelf with a little railing that keeps her from tumbling out. The aluminum door to the outside is on the right side as they face the front of the trailer. The sink, stove, refrigerator, and oven are on the same side as the door. Opposite, across a patch of vinyl floor, is the panel door to the toilet. They shower at commercial campgrounds.

Michael and Karen believe that sex is proof of their love, and it is hard for them to discern the difference. Tonight, after they are certain that Hannah is asleep, they perform quiet sex.

Although they don't talk about it, Michael and Karen feel as if they have missed the boat, that they have been cheated. They are Elvis-era puritans who'd gotten married in 1967, before the Summer of Love. When they'd wed, their marital illusions conjured Doris Day, Jimmy Stewart, and schmaltzy violins. They don't hear the violins anymore. Rifts are opening in the culture, widening along the fault lines of war, birth control, LSD, and media politics. Now there is free love – so say all the magazines and Sunday newspapers. Now, women are entitled to orgasms, don't wear bras, and do not demand marriage for sex.

Connections

The next morning, in full daylight, he is delighted by their location, a cove with enclosing red rock promontories a mile apart that gentle the warm sea between them. The nearer promontory, a few hundred yards away, looks accessible. The silhouettes of cactus, the tallest of which is way out at the end, a good quarter mile from the beach, adorn the heights. The smooth beach is undisturbed. Seabirds wheel in circles above the cove, occasionally plunging into the water to catch fish. Another rig is parked some distance away, a pickup truck with a camper top. An aluminum canoe is beached near to it, on the seaward slope of the dune. Standing atop the great mound of white sand, Michael eyes the canoe, curious about its owner.

Maybe this is what it has all been about, maybe he is not a monumental fool. Being here may, in itself, be vindication for all he's put them through. The dispossessions, dislocations and disruptions that he has inflicted upon them might actually have been worthwhile.

Hannah practices her doggy paddle as Michael and Karen stand nearby. Their daughter is enjoying herself. All is well if Hannah is doing well. She is the focus of Karen and Michael's marriage, the only aspect of their relationship they are able to talk about.

After their swim, they change into jeans and take a walk to inspect the movie set.

Joseph Heller's book, *Catch-22*, is about a Second World War bomber squadron stationed on an island in the Adriatic off of Italy. The control tower and military field offices of the movie set had been built with red-tiled, partial roofs and walls painted to look like stucco over fieldstone. The tower looks as if its top had been blown off in an explosion, spray paint artfully imitating smoke stains. That the structure is made of furring strips, canvas, and *papier maché,* rather than stone and stucco, is not apparent until they are a few feet away. The desert climate has been kind, scarcely weathering the structures.

A rough stairway attached to the back of the tower set leads to an elevated platform from which they can see over the dunes to the sea. He recognizes it as the spot where the movie characters shouted to be heard above the wind and engine noise, paying scant attention to bullet-riddled planes crashing on the runway.

Standing on the platform, Karen is impressed. "Pretty cool," she says. "It's really *Catch 22*."

For Michael, the abandoned movie set is a trash heap amidst natural magnificence - but it is actual, really here, as is the landscape. What's real? What's a fake? What's in between? What's trash? What has value? Heller's words had once been tiny ink marks on a page, then a popular novel, then they'd made a movie that had infiltrated the minds of millions more. Marks on paper, images on celluloid, thoughts, actions, consequences.

He is a connector, a network of knots between the present, the past, and the future; between fantasy and reality; between here and elsewhere; between the world and the strands of his imagination. The movie set triggers awareness of entangled abstractions that terminate in ever more tangles that compel his unraveling. He does not know how to shut it off, how to stop himself. Of late, he has tried to quell the ruminations by banishing words. He tries to see the clouds without calling them clouds, to see his shadow as merely a shape, to be in the world without naming its parts, to exist in the absence words.

"Yes," he says. "It really is."

"Is it lunchtime?" asks Hannah.

He'd undergone a change when he'd dropped acid the year before. The LSD disintegrated some of the barriers between the outside of him and his consciousness, the filters between sensation and perception. The meanings he had layered over his awareness had been like plugs in his ears, or smoke obscuring his view. He'd marveled at the undulations of a snail on the glass wall of a fish tank, seen the delicate scales and gossamer fins of his tropical fish as miracles, seen the light inside the rising bubbles as wonders. How could he not have noticed? Before the acid trip, he'd barely been conscious of the beauty and grandeur of creation. As if a new light source was shining on them, manmade objects seemed obvious, crude, simple -

ugly. Value disappeared from all the things they'd bought, all the junk they owned.

When they departed Philadelphia, they had abandoned all of their possessions inside a locker in the basement of *Creekside Apartments*, a fifty unit, garden style complex where they had prospered, paid to manage the property, a plum rent-free job that they had gladly taken to supplement his college instructor's salary. They left for Mexico after two years as the managers, having saved enough money to buy a house. But Michael doesn't want a house; he wants to use the money as living expenses while he figures out what the hell to do with his life.

He had proposed to leave Karen and Hannah with everything except the car. He'd require only enough money for his subsistence, she could keep most of what they had saved. It was best for all of them if he left to sort things out for himself. He had needed to get away.

But Karen had insisted that he take them along. He cared about them? "Well, prove it," she'd said. "Yeah, why not? Let's go. I don't like living here, with us this way, any more than you do. You want to leave? Well so do I."

It wasn't just the acid. He'd been trying to break free for years. He didn't want the life of an academic, certainly not in the field he'd entered because graduate assistants were given draft exemptions to teach the required course in public speaking. But he'd needed to quit the job, to extricate himself from a career commitment he'd made to avoid being dropped into a rice paddy and getting shot as an invader. The job had made him feel like a phony; he didn't know much about anything, yet he was supposed to be a teacher. He was a bullshit artist, a fraud who had never done anything, or gone anywhere, or knew anything worth of the cost of tuition.

The first time he tried to drop out had been when he'd completed the Master's degree requirements, a tangible accomplishment that meant he'd not wasted two years of graduate school. With the degree on his resume, and because they had replaced the draft with a lottery and he'd been given a high number, he'd felt himself free to look for a career that suited him.

But they had trapped him again by offering him a job at a branch campus in Abington, a Philadelphia suburb near Karen's and Michael's doting parents. They'd offered a full salary, tenure track, with a guarantee of a place in the PhD program as soon as he was ready to soldier on. Karen had been thrilled by the offer. His parents, her parents, were pleased that their baby granddaughter would be close by, and proud that Michael was going to be a Professor. What a joke. In reality, he knows nothing worth professing.

After the acid trip, over the course of the next few months, he began to think of people as apes wearing clothes, pretentious animals who mistook the cosmetic veneer of civilization for meaning. All the arrangements of social ordering, all the symbols of rank, all the possessions, titles, and achievements that people believed in were of no more significance than the bluster of horny baboons. We all die, no one's existence is of any greater significance than a snail's in a fish tank.

But innocent Hannah needs her parents - needs him.

Splendor

A man who Michael assumes is the owner of the truck is sitting in a folding chair at the top of the dune when they return to the trailer. Hannah and Karen go inside to shelter from the desert sun. Michael climbs the dune to introduce himself.

He's George from Colorado, a bespectacled, square-built man, here alone for the fishing.

Michael asks him if he's paying Fernando to stay.

"For all I know, he's just some *campesino* who lives around here and found a way to get some easy cash. *El guardian* has never stated a price," says George. "I just slip him a little something whenever he stops by to keep him happy."

"I gave him beer."

"Whatever works."

George makes the trip two or three times a year. He is an electrical engineer whose wife stays at home whenever George feels the need to camp behind his not-so-secret-anymore dune. He'd been hoping to have Los Algodones to himself when Michael, Karen, and Hannah Berman showed up.

"I never tell anyone about this place. They'd spoil it. You'd be amazed at some of the people I've seen here. Idiots coming in with nothing but a backpack. They make a mess of the place in no time, crapping in the bushes, leaving trash, fires all over the place. Fernando chases that sort off. How did you find out about it?"

Michael tells him about Marcel, the Frenchman who'd told him how to find Catch-22.

"Well, that's how places like this get ruined. People like him tell other people, like you, and so on and so on and, before you know it, it'll be no good for anyone anymore."

"Well, I'm glad he told me. This is an amazing place."

"You look like you know what you're doing," George says, indicating the Berman's tidy trailer and late model car.

"I do my best."

"You won't go blabbing to everybody you meet on the road, right?"

Michael denies that he would. "What kind of fish do you catch here?" he asks.

"All kinds. You name it. There's Spanish mackerel now."

"What are those like? I never caught any."

"You fish?"

"Sure. Whenever I can."

"They're fast, like little tuna. Strong."

"What do you use?"

"They'll hit anything that moves. I use buck tail. You have tackle?"

14

"I do."

"Light tackle?"

"Yep."

"Can you handle a canoe?"

"Yep."

"I go out at dawn. If you want to come along, I'll stop by when I'm ready to go. Wear a bathing suit."

///

The next morning, a dawn fog blankets the cove as George and Michael stand atop the dune. Vague, dark shapes move at the shoreline and in the surf. "Sea lions," says George.

The sun will rise above the cliffs behind them and quickly burn off the mist. "The mackerel will come right to the top when the sunlight hits the surface. We'll paddle like hell when we see a boil, paddle right through it as fast as we can. Okay?" He kneels and opens his tackle box and removes two lures made from the white hair of a deer's tail, and offers one to Michael. "You can leave your box here," he says. "You won't be needing anything I don't have. Ready?"

The dark shapes melt into the waves as the men walk down the face of the dune. They push the canoe through the quiet surf, Michael hops to the front seat, George to the back. They paddle hard for a few minutes, then quit when they are in the approximate middle of the cove. The mist around them is thin and wispy, but still too thick for the dune to be seen.

George has equipped the canoe for fishing with rod holders fashioned out of plastic electrical conduit, stiff pipes that he'd lashed to the center seat at forty five degree angles, projecting up and outward from the middle of the canoe. He'd cut a groove six inches long in the top of each pipe to accommodate the reel stems, an innovation that prevents the rods from twisting and adds a half-foot of support for the rod handles. George casts his buck tail to one side and allows it to sink then sets his rod in a holder. Michael does the same, turns and sets his rod on the other side.

The action begins when the fiery sun clears the horizon above the cliffs. The surface near the canoe erupts with small leaping fish, the topmost anchovies in dense, swirling schools that fill the cove. The agitated sea hisses with the whipping sound of their fins skittering the surface. Feeding frenzies are erupting all over the cove. Above the boils, birds wheel and plunge, their excited calls and splashes punctuating the surface hiss, sending streaks of foam into the air wherever they dive.

Michael and George take up the paddles and start into the nearest boil. Michael feels the canoe jerk before their third stroke. Their reels click, then chatter as the drag gears slow the unspooling lines. He grabs his rod from its holder and pulls its tip back to sense the size of whatever had mistaken the streamer for the flashing side of its prey, to see how the rod bends, to feel the weight, to test the fighting spirit of a wild thing.

The mackerel he hoists out of the sea is a bit less than two feet long, sleek and muscular, a tuna in elongated miniature, blue on top with vivid blue-green tiger stripes zigzagging down its silver sides. It is big-eyed, pointy-finned, sharp-toothed, and beautiful. Michael unhooks a half dozen of the fish during the feeding frenzy, releasing all but the first. Many get away before he can retrieve them. Toward the end, after the sun has risen enough to light the clear waters to a depth, he sees that every mackerel he reels toward the surface is followed by a much larger fish that George identifies as a species called jack crevalle. Below the jacks, larger shapes swim.

When the surface calms, when the sun's angle no longer makes beacons of the anchovies, they paddle to shore. Michael cleans the mackerel and builds a cooking fire of mesquite wood on the lee of the dune. Karen cuts a lime to squeeze on the dark oily meat, and cuts Hannah's pieces to make sure there are no bones.

///

George leaves for Colorado, as planned, the following morning. As he is leaving, he drives by their trailer and pauses to say goodbye. Michael reaches through the open window to shake his hand.

"Thanks again. It was great. I'll never forget it."

"It was nice to meet you," says George. "Take care, now. And remember – wherever you go, there you are."

The Welders of Guaymas

On the morning they plan to depart Catch-22, a week later, Michael discovers the broken hitch. With all their gear readied for a day on the road, as Karen and Hannah watch, he can't get the trailer's hitch socket to attach to the steel ball protruding from the back of the car. Normally, he accomplishes this by turning a crank that lowers the front of the trailer onto the ball. This time, there is no resistance to the weight of the trailer as he cranks it down. He looks under the car and sees the hitch contraption dangling from the driver side of the car chassis. Apparently, the attachment bolts have come loose. He recalls some jarring bounces on the dirt track from the main road during their ride to Catch-22 and assumes that's when the damage occurred. The bolts on the passenger side still hold, so he will be able to drive the car without dragging the hitch.

They have no choice but to postpone their departure until the damage is repaired. They will have to go in search of someone who can reattach the hitch. But there is no point to schlepping Hannah around with them as they search a foreign town for someone capable of the job. So they decide that Karen will remain with Hannah, and Michael will go the the nearest town, Guaymas, and see what can be done. If it requires more than a few hours to get it repaired, he'll make an appointment with the shop for the next day. In either case, he will definitely be back by suppertime. Michael retrieves the Spanish/English dictionary he keeps inside the trailer and finds *soldador*, the word for "welder."

He drives off, leaving Hannah and Karen alone, going very slowly along the dirt track for a couple of miles until he reaches the paved highway. He goes right, heading south to the city of Guaymas, pronounced with a very soft 'G', fifteen miles away.

Alone at the wheel, he thinks about Hannah. She often sucks her thumb, and when she does, he sees her eyes wander inside herself. She's a good kid – obedient, rarely acting out. It's what she does when she is not drawing, or eating, or playing with her toys. It's something about her during the intervals between activities that concerns him. She doesn't wait well.

But, of course, she's only four years old and time is a new thing to comprehend. So they are at that stage of family development when Michael and Karen try to organize her attention. The backseat of the car is her domain, with diversions spread around her. They even have a back-seat TV with a black and white eight-inch screen that runs off the car battery or off the trailer's electrical system when they are inside. They all miss her friends on *Sesame Street*. Deep in Sonora's semi-arid landscape of widespread settlements, they can only get fuzzy Mexican soap operas.

He'd noticed roadside repair yards on the outskirts of the towns through which they'd traveled on the way to Los Algodones. Guaymas appears from the map to be a city, the largest they have encountered since they'd crossed the border at Tijuana. And, as he'd hoped, he comes across a place with car parts arrayed around a small yellow building with an open garage door. There are no signs out front, but there can be no doubt about the purpose of the place; a truck and a car have their hoods open; engines and transmission parts lay strewn about on the gravel and dust of the roadside. He passes slowly, pulls onto the shoulder, parks, and walks back to the repair yard.

A man comes out of the dark garage into the bright sunlight and approaches.

"Buenas dias," Michael says.

"*Buenah,*" says the man

"Yo tengo una problema con mi auto-mobi-le," he says, feeling a fool. "Yo necessito uno soldador."

Back at the car, he pushes down on the hitch ball as the man watches. "Es el problema," Michael says.

The man gets onto his belly and looks under the car. He reaches up and tests the dangling hitch bar. He stands up and says he can fix it, "*Si. Lo puedo arreglar,*" he says, cleaning his palms on his pant legs.

Michael knows the word for "where." He asks, "Donde? Aqui?"

"Si. Aqui."

When? "Cuando? Ahora?"

"Si. Ahora."

You can do this? "Usted?"

"Si.

"Que es su nombre?" asks Michael. It's good to know a man's name. At the least, he hopes to gain a little sympathy.

"My name's Pedro... Pete," says the mechanic, smiling slyly. "I speak English."

"Thank goodness. Hi. My name's Mike Berman, I'm from Philadelphia."

"Pete Espinozo, from Arizona."

"Very glad to meet you," says Michael.

Dean and Remus

Karen is pleased that Michael is gone. His outsized personality demands attention all the time. They are amicable together, for Hannah's sake. But now she and Hannah are by themselves for the first time in weeks, and it feels good.

They are inside the trailer, the music of *Willy Wonka and The Chocolate Factory* is playing on their portable tape player. Hannah is at the drop-down table with her coloring book and two Barbie Dolls.

They hear crunching tires and the sound of a big engine. They look through the windows at an enormous recreational vehicle, an arvee, pulling into the space that George's pickup camper had occupied.

"Uh oh," says Hannah.

"There's nothing to worry about," says Karen. "It's just a *Winnebago*."

The little girl puts thumb to mouth and watches the door of the bus, waiting to see what sort of people occupy a behemoth.

"Let's go say hello, shall we?" says Karen.

They leave the trailer and are halfway to the arvee when its door opens and a black Labrador Retriever leaps to the ground, followed by a man in his late twenties wearing a khaki tee shirt, blue jeans, cowboy boots, and a

Stetson hat. The dog dashes to the crest of the dune. The man smiles broadly and waves in their direction, then follows the dog. He climbs with short, controlled steps, as if he's had practice climbing sandy hills, halts at the top, and looks out over the Gulf of California. He lifts his hat with one hand, runs the fingers of the other through a mop of blonde curls, and replaces the hat. He looks over his shoulder to Karen and Hannah below and says, "Wow!"

The dog scampers down the dune and starts sniffing the terrain, darting from bush to dent, snuffling with pleasure, then charges back up the dune to join his master, who strides several yards in each direction, the dog leaping ahead, enjoying the softness of the white sand. After a minute or so, the man spreads his arms for balance and bounds down the dune to the flattened red ground. He walks toward Karen and Hannah.

"Hi," he says. "This is some kind of place."

Karen returns his smile. "Oh, yeah," she says. "Are you going to camp here?"

"Abso - goddam - lutely," he says. "Who do I have to pay?"

"Fernando. He works at the ranchero. He'll be around later."

"What do they charge?"

Karen shrugs. "You'll have to work that out with Fernando. We'll be leaving soon."

"My name's Dean. This is Remus."

"How is he around children?"

"Fine. Go ahead, Remus. Go say 'hi'."

The dog walks calmly toward them, snuffs Karen's outstretched hand, then sits down next to Hannah as if she is an old friend, his glossy black flank only inches from the little girl.

Hannah touches the dog's shoulder. When he appears not to mind, she touches him with both hands, pushing her fingers through his warm coat. "He likes me," she says.

"I think he does. You must be a very nice person," says Dean.

"Yes. I am very nice," says Hannah.

"Remus likes to go swimming. Would you like to watch him swim?"

"Yes."

Dean says, "Now, Remus. Swim!"

The dog cocks his head, rises from his haunches and dashes up the dune, followed by the people. Indeed, Remus loves to swim. By the time the humans top the dune, he's already beyond the mild surf, paddling merrily toward the horizon.

"Remus," Dean hollers, "Come."

Karen is amazed that the dog circles back and swims toward shore. "He's so well behaved," she says.

"We're working on it," says Dean. "What's your name?"

"Karen Berman. And this is Hannah. My husband, his name's Michael, went to town to get our hitch fixed."

"Well, hi," he says, and extends his large hand. Her eyes rest for a moment on a tanned, heavily muscled arm covered with fine blond hair. She shakes his hand, sensing hard strength under a gentle grip. "Y'all been here very long?" he asks.

"About a week. We were going to leave this morning. Then the hitch broke."

"Mommy, can I go swimming with Remus?"

"I don't know," says Karen.

"Remus would be glad for the company," says Dean. "I'll watch him."

They hurry back to the trailer. Hannah runs ahead and changes into her bathing suit. It's midday, the sun intense, and Karen makes sure the child-size safari cap is tied under Hannah's chin before she allows her to run back to the beach.

Hannah runs into the gentle surf, belly flops in the shallows, gets to her feet, and bounces to an area of waist-deep water where she can run and practice swimming close to her mother. The dog is headed out to sea.

Dean puts a hand to his mouth and whistles. The dog responds and swims toward shore. When he is at the same depth as Hannah, the cowboy holds his palm up and says, "Okay."

Remus woofs in acknowledgment, pleased to know his assignment. Thereafter, he doesn't stray far from the little girl, as if he's responsible for her. Hannah is delighted, and Remus seems content to swim in circles around her.

"Your dog is amazing," says Karen. "He seems to understand, like a person."

"Not always. Like I said, we work on it."

"It's just you and him?"

"Just me and Remus."

"That's a big *Winnebago*," she says.

Karen and Michael are minimalists, offended by excess. A *Winnebago* uses a lot more gasoline than the Berman's six-cylinder sedan. Big motor homes like the kind Dean is driving are usually owned by middle- aged retirees from the Midwest, not by handsome cowboys in tee shirts.

They'd bought their car the year before. Their dropout, this whole Mexico idea, had sprung to Michael's mind shortly after he began driving that car. The son of a bitch! Not so fast, buster.

Where the hell is Michael? When is he coming back?

The Weld

P ete summons two men from the dark interior of the yellow building and explains the job to them. They do the work outside, raising the car three feet off the ground by driving it up ramps onto platforms. They bring an oxygen and an acetylene tank from the garage on a hand truck and stand them next to the car. Pete covers his face with a welder's mask, takes a loop of thick wire and the torch, lies on his back, and slides underneath the car.

As he watches, Michael thinks about the only other mishap they had suffered since they began their journey. It had occurred the month before and now, as he thinks about it, he considers the possibility that the other incident might have been the original cause of the cracked bolts. They had been struck from behind during a traffic jam as they drove into Los Angeles on Interstate 5.

They had crossed the country in five days, spending nights at trailer parks in Ohio, Missouri, Colorado and Nevada. Michael had planned the first leg as a shake-down cruise before entering Mexico, a safe time on good roads with ready access to gas stations and supermarkets. Guided by a *KOA* campground location index, a *Rand McNally* road atlas, and a *Triple-A* itinerary, the trip had been smooth until they hit the I-5 in Los Angeles. Stuck in more traffic then he'd ever seen, they were bumped from behind, just a nudge that barely propelled their car forward an inch or two. Welcome to LA.

"Jesus!" Karen said, twisting in the passenger seat to see whether Hannah was alright. "Are you okay?"

"What the hell was that?" said seat-belted Hannah, surrounded by her coloring books, drawing tools and dolls.

Michael had eased off the brakes, listened to the engine, wiggled the wheel. When a few yards of traffic opened up ahead of them, he filled the space, attentive to the heft and angle of the trailer pushing from behind when he braked, watching the wing mirrors to see whether the impact had knocked the trailer askew. He'd heard no grinding, felt nothing amiss. He'd set the hand brake, shifted into neutral gear, stepped out of the car, and walked to the rear of the rig to see the damage, aware that he was potential road kill.

He'd looked through the windshield of the pickup truck immediately behind the trailer, no doubt the vehicle that had hit them. The man at the wheel ignored his gaze, pretending that nothing involving him had occurred. Michael thrust both hands into the air, palms up, glaring at the other driver. The jerk deserved to be confronted, but to what end? They were only a few miles from their destination at the end of the first leg. While it might have been satisfying to confront him, to call him an idiot, to collect his insurance information, and so on, it would have served no practical purpose. Instead, he'd returned to the wheel of the *Dodge*.

He had not noticed the missing bumper cap. The impact had popped the rubber cap off the long, hollow bumper at the back of the trailer inside of which the sewer hose was stowed. Perhaps he might have noticed the open end of the bumper right after the accident happened had he been less conscious of the steel stampede surrounding his soft body, each lethal vehicle in the eight lanes of the I-5 under the control of someone impatient to be somewhere else.

As specified in the *Triple-A* itinerary on Karen's lap, the exit they were to take had been only a mile ahead of them. As Michael steered off the I-5, to their friends' house in Hollywood, tension in the car softened, each of the Bermans relieved to be out of the traffic.

Surprisingly, Hollywood is a real place. Michael had recognized the bungalow style of the houses, the squared lawns, the play of sunlight and shadows, the wide streets, and the palm trees. Keystone Cops might careen around any corner, Technicolor movie stars might stroll along a sidewalk.

Ted and Bea Silver had invited them to stay at their house and use it as the base from which to stage their journey to Mexico. They'd been expecting the Bermans arrival, and came out of the house to greet them as Michael pulled to a stop at the curb. After hugs all around,

Michael steered the trailer backward into the driveway on the third try.

He'd told Ted what had occurred on the Interstate. "I didn't really get a good look at the damage."

"You got out of the car? On the I-5?"

"For a few seconds."

A spare tire mounted above the bumper is the rear-most piece of the rig, thus the part that must have been struck. Inspecting the tire with Ted, he'd seen two faint creases on either side of the rim – the point of impact. But it is possible, Michael now believes, that the sudden force had damaged one of the hitch bolts, perhaps causing a hairline crack, that snapped on the way into Los Algodones. When one bolt was broken, it put more stress on the other two on the same side, and all three snapped.

He already knew of one bad consequence – the loss of a sewer hose. A week after the incident on the I-5, they'd been at a gas station near Yosemite. As he had been filling the tank, a woman pulled up at the other pump and informed him that some "long snaky thing" had been dangling out of the back of his trailer, until it fell out completely, and rolled onto the road shoulder miles back. She had honked her horn, to get his attention, she'd said. That had been when he'd realized that the impact on the I-5 had popped the rubber cap off the bumper.

It is at this point that he commits a tragic error. Michael wants Pete to reinforce the joint by welding a strip of metal over it. And he wants the same done on the other side.

"It's good the way it is, believe me," says Pete. "You don't need any more."

"Listen, Pete, the trailer and this car is all I've got. Me, my wife and our little girl, we live in it. We have a long way to go and I don't want to take any chances."

"I'm not sure it's a good idea," says Pete.

"I'll pay for it."

"That's not the issue," says the man from Arizona. "There's a reason why they don't weld trailer hitches on-to a little chassis like this one."

"What's the risk?"

Pete shrugs. "I don't know. But they don't recommend it."

"I can't see what harm it can do."

"Well, if it's what you want."

"Please," says Michael.

And so he stands by as one of the helpers retrieves some strips of quarter inch steel from the garage. Pete gets back under the car to reinforce the bond according to the *gringo's* wish.

"It's as strong as it can get," says Pete when he emerges the second time.

"Thanks," says Michael. "You're sure? Can we test it?"

One of the helpers gets behind the wheel and backs the car down the ramps to the dry earth. Pete says something to the other guy, a roly-poly fellow who obligingly walks to the back of the car and steps onto the hitch ball, balancing himself with his hands on the deck of the trunk. Grinning, he bounces up and down a few times, proving the strength of the weld.

They all laugh at the sight that Michael will never forget.

Nap Time

Karen is cautious about their food and water. They have heard stories about Montezuma's Revenge and fill their twenty-five gallon tank only from big glass bottles of filtered *Agua Pura*. They avoid restaurants, relying on packaged foods from the *Super Mercado.* They disinfect fruits and vegetables by soaking them in a light bleach solution. So far, since they crossed into Mexico, they have been healthy.

After Hannah's swim, Karen returns with her to the trailer and towels her dry. The little girl puts her clothes on and combs her hair by herself. She climbs onto the cushioned bench at the drop-down table to eat a sandwich of sliced ham, hopefully safe, as it comes refrigerated in plastic wrap. The bread is packaged too, white and sliced, just like back in the States. Hannah likes to twirl her thin blond hair with her fingers. She would like her hair to be longer and thicker, like Barbie's.

"Use both hands, please," says Karen.

They aren't used to Michael's absence. He is the one-in-charge, competent, focused – father, husband, and discovery guide who is as likely to enthuse over the shape of a tree, as over a hit movie, or a ride at *Disneyland,* or how good the food tastes. Some of that is for Hannah's benefit, she knows. He wants the child to experience what they find around them fearlessly - whereas Karen is alert for risks. They are a whole, Karen and Michael the *yin* and *yang* of parenting, their child is the *Tao*.

But Michael is dissatisfied with his wife; at some point the marriage will end. It is inevitable. She knows it's coming. But she is not ready.

They'd gotten married the month she graduated from college. For a year, they'd lived in a walkup apartment in Center City Philadelphia. She'd had a job that year, qualifying applicants for child welfare. Then Michael quit his school teacher job to take an assistantship at Penn State. It had been 1967, when the war in Vietnam had been sucking every young man into the bloody jungle. The job as a teaching graduate assistant had come with a draft exemption.

Karen was admitted to the Audiology graduate school and was initially enthusiastic about the field. But, once she became pregnant, her attentions turned more personal than academic or professional. Unlike Michael, she had not completed the degree requirements. How could she take a job, even if anyone would hire her, and take care of Hannah? No, she needed the marriage in order to keep a roof over their heads.

But that didn't mean that it would never end. It had too. They weren't good for each other. She knows that. But who would be good for her? What kind of man would she prefer to Michael? Would such a man even be interested in her?

She takes a book and one of their aluminum folding chairs to the top of the dune. She's wearing a white cotton shirt loosely over a black tank suit. She looks good in a bathing suit, she has nice legs and she's still as fit as she had been on her high school's swim and cheerleading teams. She opens the book, and squints to the Western horizon.

She can't concentrate on the book. The dazzling light of the noonday sun bounces off the sea onto her face, a force of nature that demands her attention.

She doesn't know how to make Michael happy. Whatever he wants from her, she hasn't been able to deliver it. He claims to be satisfied with their sex; he certainly likes it. He always wants them to do it, taking every opportunity when they are alone. But, as far as she is concerned, it could be much better. He suggests that they try things, different positions and all that, but she never makes suggestions. She complies with his wishes, which are modest, and never minds his attention. But she is a disappointed lover, and that disappoints him.

But it's not only the sex. Their perceptions are not synchronized. He is preoccupied by the unseen - everything means something else, which means something else, which implies something else, and so on, and so on. She never knows what odd insight, what skewed observation, what convoluted opinion he will articulate. It's not that she has no interest in abstraction – she can be as intellectual as the situation requires. It's rather that she does it only when necessary, whereas he ponders everything all the time. He's interesting, but exhausting.

The biggest issue is the uncertainty. He's not a doctor or a lawyer, he has no job, and doesn't know what job he wants. He's considering his options, but has not narrowed them down. "I think I'm a writer," he says. "I think that's what I can do."

Yeah. But how will we live?

She hears the door to the *Winnebago* open and close. Over her shoulder, she sees Remus charge up the dune and come to a stop facing her, as if to say Hi.

"Hello, Remus," she says.

The light reflecting on water dazzles her, washing colors pale. Sitting atop a sand dune surrounded by open horizons, she's disoriented, almost dizzy. She hears Dean's voice. He's standing at the base of the dune with two bottles of beer dangling from the fingers of one hand.

He grins. "Thirsty?" he offers.

Money

Their ultimate destination is the City of Oaxaca, two-thousand miles south-south-east of Los Algodones. They intend to look for a good trailer park once they arrive and stay indefinitely. They will travel south along the Pacific Coast most of the way, staying at campgrounds, then cut inland and south. The trailer parks charge around five dollars a night. Michael expects that the journey to Oaxaca will take a couple of weeks, with a few days in Mexico City to see the sights, and a final day to drive three-hundred miles south of the capitol to Oaxaca.

They have agreed on Oaxaca, pronounced *wuh-HOK-a*, on the basis of guidebooks. It's a modern, mountain city near pre-Columbian ruins. There are villages in the surrounding valleys where people craft inexpensive objects that Michael might be able to resell in the States. They have a destination and a mission.

There is a problem with the mission; Michael does not like buying and he is an awkward salesman. He's had sales jobs from time to time and discovered that he doesn't like persuading people to part with their money

As for buying, he's mindful of pennies. The money they'd saved is in an American bank, an account on which he can write traveler's checks. He doesn't know how long the money will last, perhaps a year. It depends on how much they spend: on whether they choose to invest in trade goods, on whether they encounter emergencies that require money. He thinks of the money in terms of days - each day not clocking hours for a paycheck is a day of freedom. It's not the money he hoards – it's the freedom.

He suspects that he's been bullshitting himself about the export business. He's sure it's feasible, but he's not been able to imagine a life devoted to buying and selling. Nonetheless, the notion has been useful, providing them with a mission and a destination. He and Karen will sort things out, make the big decisions, allow the real problems to ripen until the right choice – ending the marriage - becomes obvious. She will have to let him go.

Bullshit is his area of expertise. He'd spent six years listening to undergraduates fulfill the University's mandatory public speaking requirement - he's heard a lot of bullshit. Worse, he had to provide commentary about every presentation – bullshit about the bullshit. On top of all of that, his job was to teach rhetoric, lecture on how to structure thoughts as words in order to achieve a purpose: to inform, to entertain, or to persuade - more bullshit about bullshit. He'd taught the required Speech course for three years as a graduate assistant, and three more as a full-time Instructor at the branch campus. He calculates that he'd endured one-thousand-eight- hundred presentations during those six years.

Had he wanted to, he could have spent the rest of his life teaching Speech 200. He'd shown up every day, listened, taught, listened, listened and listened some more. The job had been easy, so he'd also demanded written work in the form of tests and term papers so that he had enough to do when he wasn't in the classroom.

The job had required him to identify the strengths and weaknesses in each of the five-to-ten minute presentations, all one-thousand-eight-hundred of them. Were they supported by evidence, testimony, or example? Were they clearly organized? Did they have objectives? Simple stuff that, frustratingly, was only occasionally delivered. Day after day, staying optimistic, careful to stay professional and impersonal, class after class, year after year for six years, he had dissected the bullshit. That's what he'd been paid to do.

But he hadn't chosen to become a professor of bullshit; it had been shelter from the storm of American militarism. As soon as he'd been officially informed that he would receive the Masters degree, shortly after the Government replaced the draft with a lottery and he'd gotten lucky with a high number, he had announced his intention not to pursue the doctorate. He'd made up his mind to quit. Then, even though he hadn't asked for it and didn't want it, the University offered him a job that was so good he couldn't refuse it, especially since Karen was pregnant with Hannah

The degree itself was well-earned and legitimate, he'd written a pretty good thesis about Malcolm X's rhetoric, potentially useful if he decided to pursue a doctorate. Those were his fallbacks; a Social Studies teaching certificate from the State of Pennsylvania and an M.A. from the State University. He knew that he could always earn money one way or another; work is work and a dollar is a dollar. He had been collecting pay for work since the age of twelve, taking any sort of job: summer jobs, sales jobs, menial jobs. He'd do anything anyone paid him to do.

The pay for teaching Speech 200 had been enough for a young family to live on. The opportunity to save money came when they took on second jobs as the resident managers of the apartment complex where they'd lived. Along with a weekly salary, that in itself was enough to live on, they'd been given an apartment with rent and utilities paid by the absentee owner of a fifty unit complex of garden apartments in Elkins Park, a neighborhood two miles from the campus. He'd changed washers, made sure every rent check was paid, kept the books, mowed the grass, and so on. He and Karen did the jobs for two years, she answering the phone and making necessary calls when he was away on campus. So they had saved all of his teaching salary for two years.

Michael spurns luxury, buying only what they need, no more. He is not into cars. When he'd been given money for the specific purpose of buying a new car, he'd chosen the most reliable one for which funds were available. The *1972 Dodge Dart*, powered by a tilted rack of six cylinders, the famously sturdy *Slant Six* engine. But the notion of using it to pull a trailer had not occurred to him as he'd been choosing what to do with his grandfather's car money. That had been Karen's idea.

His father's father died two years after he took the job in Abington. The notion of a deeply depressed old man who spoke broken English, who called a car a *machine*, specifying that his assets be redistributed as automobiles, struck Michael as out of character. The car was his parents' gift, not his grandfather's.

Years before, Michael's father, Henry, announced that Grandpop would reward Michael's older brother, Steve, with a *Cadillac* when he graduated from medical school, but the car never materialized. Michael suspected that their father had never even mentioned the promise to their grandfather. After the old man died and Michael's parents pondered how to spend the miniscule fortune he'd left them, they decided to make good on a promise the old man had never made. Michael's mother insisted that if Steve was to get a car, then so too was Michael.

Michael had taken possession of the car after Thanksgiving, 1972. In January, he'd announced his intention to resign from the teaching job as of the end of the 1973 Spring Term. The car's potential to go as far as the roads would take him had changed everything, tipped the scales, making escape seem possible.

Karen had resisted - she and Hannah were coming with him wherever he wanted to go, but they weren't going to live in a tent. Could the *Dodge* pull a trailer? Yes, as it turned out, but just a little one.

The fateful roadside repair takes but half an hour - there's more than enough daylight left to return to Catch-22, hitch up, and cover over a hundred miles. He hands Pete cash for the welding job.

Pulling into the road, he decides to turn right, to head south and scout Guaymas on his own. Karen and Hannah will be just fine without him for another hour or so.

He is as free as he has ever been.

Back at the Ranchero

Hannah awakes from her nap and climbs down from her bunk bed, carefully dropping to the the bench cushion, then onto the the vinyl floor of their trailer. Where's Mommy? She opens the screen door, and there she is, her mother, outside, sitting on top of the dune with the *Winnebago* man. Hannah gets into her yellow sun dress, leaves the trailer, and goes up the hill to be with her mother.

Remus is swimming, paddling around for the fun of it. He is so nice, like a friend. Even better… he's a dog. They don't stay anywhere long enough for her to have friends to play with. Trailer parks and campgrounds are her world now; she hardly ever sees kids her age. She tries to make friends. A couple of times, the other kids have hurt her feelings.

Mommy and the *Winnebago* man are talking.

Mommy says, "We're heading to Oaxaca."

The man is sitting cross-legged on the sand next to Mommy at the top of the dune, with his knees pointing out, his elbows on his thighs, and his hands on the ankles of his boots. "Me too," he says. "How about that."

"Well… isn't that something," says Mommy, using that tone of voice that means she's considering something. But she's smiling a little bit, as if she likes the idea.

"Yeah. That's something," says the man. He is interesting to look at. He's bigger than Daddy. He asks Mommy a question, "Why are you going to Oaxaca?"

Her mother lifts her arms from the chair rests, twists around to look at the *Winnebago* man, and says, "We hear it's nice. We have the time, so we thought we'd check it out."

"So you're on vacation?"

"Sort of. More like a quest."

The man turns away from looking at Mommy and faces the wide ocean, bright under the desert sun. He stiffens his neck and tugs the brim of his cowboy hat, bringing it low to shade his eyes. "A quest?" he asks.

"Something like that," says Mommy. "We just dropped out. I guess we're looking for a job. Or something. Maybe a business opportunity. I don't know. But Oaxaca sounds like a good place to go looking for it."

"Good for you," says the man.

"Yeah," says Mommy. "Good for us. Why are you going to Oaxaca?"

"I'm meeting someone there. An old friend of mine… he lives there."

"So what kind of business are you in?"

The man leans back with both of his hands in the sand. He says, "Well, to tell you the truth, I'm kind of between jobs. I just got out of the Army. The *Winnebago's* not mine - I'm delivering it to this guy in Oaxaca."

Mommy says, "That's cool. You were over there? In Vietnam?"

"Where else? But I'm out of it now."

Mommy leans back in her chair and looks at Hannah. "How you doin', Kiddo?"

Hannah says, "Can I go swimming with Remus?"

"I think Remus is getting tired," the man says. "He'll be coming out soon."

"For his supper?" Hannah asks.

"I guess so," says the man. "A dog's got to eat."

"What does Remus eat?"

"Dog food."

"From a can?"

"That is all correct, young lady. You're pretty smart aren't you?"

Hannah puts her thumb in her mouth.

"Hannah!" Mommy says, and she realizes that she's doing it again. Daddy doesn't like her to suck her thumb. Mommy is more forgiving. But not now.

"Remus! Come!" says the *Winnebago* man.

Hannah is drawn to animals. But they cannot have a pet. They used to have a fish tank. Daddy had left the tank bubbling in the apartment when they'd left, the man who was going to be living there would be taking care of them. The thing about dogs is that they like people. But Daddy says be cautious. But not with Remus! He is so friendly. He wags his tail when she says his name. He wants to play, plunging his forepaws into the sand and pivoting to be chased. She obliges, laughing. Then he turns and charges her, speeding past her close enough that she tags him, and it's her turn to chase him. They play this game on both sides of the dune and at the water's edge. What fun!

Locating The Tao

In Guaymas, he drives past a market square and a church until he reaches a cluster of buildings near the docks. As always, he's at the end of a road; wherever he goes, there he is. He parks at a curb off the market square, gets out of the car, locks it, opens the trunk, and retrieves the book he'd bought in Los Angeles, the *I Ching,* a dense translation of an ancient Chinese book, a Taoist tome of divination and puzzling wisdom.

He's hungry. Back at the trailer, he'd have a sterile ham sandwich, the safest food they could find. Here, the aromas of boiling beans and sizzling goat fat scent the air. He cannot resist the allure of a table in front of one of the restaurants across the street from a seawall. He'll watch the pelicans and have a meal.

Birdlife is abundant. Dark flocks roost in the trees of the town square, scavengers strut on rooftops and perch on pilings, hunters soar high and dive hard into the sea. He knows their names, cannot keep them from sneaking into his mind; *blackbird, albatross and frigate bird - the pelicans and the terns.*

The lady from inside the restaurant comes out and asks what he'll have, and he orders grilled meat wrapped in tortillas with onions, beans, and a beer.

An Anglo woman in her twenties walks along the quay, passes Michael, and continues another slow, thirty yards on the sidewalk to the end of the block, scrutinizing the restaurants. She lingers at the street corner and stands facing his direction. She is wearing an ankle-length dress and carries a big straw bag. She is tall and tanned, with dark hair chopped short. When two men rise to vacate their table at the restaurant next to his, she moves to take it.

He has a tendency to seek eye contact with strangers, especially women. It's bad manners, he knows, but he is compulsively curious and has the naiveté of a person who finds everyone interesting. With women, his curiosity is laced with the instinctive hope of a teenage boy, that one of them will look into his eyes and immediately say, 'let's go fuck'. But it's bad manners to stare, so he opens the book as the woman approaches and pretends that he does not notice when she sits down at a table only a few yards away from his.

His introduction to Taoism had been a Speech-To-Inform delivered by a one-armed Vietnam veteran, an undergraduate as old as he, returned form the war. It had been a pleasantly surprising presentation, as he'd never heard of Taoism before the guy delivered the speech. He'd given him an 'A.' A day or so later, he'd gotten a memo to remove the student's name, which he couldn't recall, from the class roll. He'd kept an eye out for awhile after the speech, hoping to see him on campus, wanting to know a little more about Taoism, curious about the way the man connected war and his wounds with a philosophy, but the guy never reappeared.

Then he'd seen references to two ancient Chinese books cited in *The Whole Earth Catalog*, a folio-sized, soft-covered book with a striking picture of Earth from space on its cover. Inside were assorted topics in tiny print, new age stuff not addressed in mainstream publications. It turned out that his friend Ted, in whose house they'd stayed before entering Mexico, had a copy of one of them, *The I Ching*, a translation subtitled in English as *The Book of Change*. Michael started reading it and was soon enthralled by its geometries and almost meaningful text. He bought a copy of it and another book, *The Tao-Te-Ching* by Lao Tzu at a bookstore the day before they'd left, but had not opened either one since they had crossed the border.

It is the dawning of the Age of Aquarius, when people are still stunned by what they'd learned in the 1960s. In 1973, the radio plays heavy rock music. Bookshops and magazine counters feature stories about communes, hippies, sexual revolution, Richard Nixon, and LSD.

The woman in the long dress has a book of her own. She looks up and he cannot stop himself from trying to make eye contact. They look back to their books. But he's aware of her, as he eats a *carnita* and washes it down with the good local beer.

The Tao is a way, like a path that must be walked to be understood, but cannot be walked unless it is understood. The idea that opposites coexist in a harmony that comes with understanding, that one should identify opposites and seek the balance between them, strikes him as absolutely true. Too, he finds the logical impossibilities delicious. Now, for example, as always, he is at the end of the path, because the path of Tao is the end, the destination and the journey are inseparable. Wonderful! Every path dead-ends in the moment. The discipline he's trying to master is to hold the moments long enough to love them.

The woman in the long dress is still eating when the restaurant lady asks him if he wants something else. He is a restless person, who eats quickly and usually wants to be on his way as soon as he wipes his lips. But not today. He asks, por favor, for a cup of tea. Perhaps he can strike up a conversation with the woman if he times his departure with hers.

And so it is that, when he sees her rising to leave her table, he leaves the shade of the umbrella and stands in the afternoon sun on the sidewalk and waits for her to come within speaking distance. She carries her bag on a shoulder strap made of soft wool yarns. The long dress disguises her form, only the skin of her face and hands is exposed. She averts her eyes as she nears, looking down to shift the book from her hand into her bag, but he isn't able to read the title.

And then she looks down at the book in his hand.

Obligingly, he shows her the cover. "I don't know how to pronounce it," he says. "But it's really interesting."

She stops in midstride, glances at his face, reaches into her purse, and removes a pair of sunglasses. She puts them on and returns his gaze, her eyes obscured by the dark glass. But she does not walk on, and they stand, face to face.

"I think it's 'yee jing'," she says.

"Thanks," he replies. "Do you know the book?"

"I've looked at it," she says.

"What did you think?"

She looks at him, but does not speak.

Unconsciously, he smiles. "Sorry," he says. "That's a bad habit. I used to be a teacher; sometimes I forget that life's not a quiz."

As if he's pushed her, she takes a step back.

The seabirds leave their perches and fly toward the water.

Keeping It Together

When Michael tried persuading her to agree to divorce, before she'd even been pregnant, Karen had asked him why, and he'd said that he wasn't sure, that he did not know, that he was just unhappy in the marriage and wanted out. But, even though he's never said it, it means that she isn't good enough. It has something to do with their sex life, with which he's obsessed. The good part about it is that so long as Michael gets his regular dose, he's fine - he doesn't complain or criticize. But she knows that he wants more from her.

Michael is the only lover she's had. At first, during her sophomore year, when they'd started dating, it had been exciting: sneaking gropes in the shadows. Then, after they'd been dating for a couple of months, sensing that the time would soon come when she'd have to *do it* to keep him interested, she'd obtained a prescription for The Pill from the campus clinic. They'd come home from college on a break between terms, and in her bedroom, while her parents were off at a concert, they'd had sex. He's been obsessed by it ever since, his ardor unabated, whispered gasps punctuating his efforts before he rolls away to his side of the bed. She finds it pleasant, never thrilling, always messy. She doesn't welcome post-coital cuddling.

Michael had once brought home a copy of *The Joy of Sex*, an illustrated, sensationally popular best seller that was subtitled *A Gourmet Guide to Lovemaking*. It features artful line drawings of a trendy couple with all their parts showing - caressing, sucking, licking, and copulating in different positions. The text treats sex as if it is like cooking and serving tasty meals. He had urged her to read it with him. She'd thumbed through it once when he'd first shown it to her, but not since.

But now she is on a beach, alone, save for a child, a dog, and a handsome cowboy. For the first time in her life, the sight of a man excites her. The pictures she'd seen in the book must have soaked into her mind, despite the fact that she'd been repelled by them when Michael had first shown them to her. Now, as she busies Hannah with her Barbie dolls and her coloring books, she thinks of a penis and a woman opened to receive it.

And where the hell is Michael? How far must he have traveled to find someone to make the repair? When would he be back?

This man in the *Winnebago* is flirting with her.

Where the hell is Michael?

Patience Monroe

The dress covering the woman drapes the tips of her breasts and falls to her ankles. She opens her bag and peers inside it, then closes it, and backs another step away from him. From this distance, he finds her beautiful.

"Are you all right?" he says.

"I am," she says. "But this is just weird." She reaches into the bag and slowly removers her book, and then shows it to him, her copy of the *I Ching*.

"I'll be damned," he says.

"It's too strange," she says.

She removes the sunglasses and peers at him. Her eyes are like wells descending to a deep place where things worth knowing lie. A primal dance begins - a man and woman are alone together, claiming their space, looking for that undulating, soft boundary, the one that's palpable when lust invades. It's a fine veil, a form of the Tao. If touched, fingertip to fingertip, it is perfect and exquisite.

But he senses that he's pushing too hard, and he withdraws. He says, "I want to watch the birds." He turns away, checks both ends of the street for traffic, crosses to the seawall, leans his hips into the barrier, and watches the hungry birds. They are attacking the schools of silver anchovies swirling upward to escape the mackerel and jacks attacking from below. Poor fish. He feels her presence next to him, but does not turn his eyes away from the glory on the water.

"I want to talk about it," she says.

"Me too," he says. "You are the only other person I've ever met who's read it. I am a little afraid of it."

"Afraid? Of what?"

"I've never done it," he says. "I've never asked it a question and tossed the coins. I've just read bits of it, the *Introduction* all the way through, and I've looked at the meanings that are written for some of the hexagrams, but I haven't actually used it."

"Why not?"

"Mainly because I don't know how to ask the question."

If you toss three coins together six times, and you record the number of heads or tails in each toss as either a straight heads line (———————), or a broken tails line (——— ———), you draw a stack of six lines, some combination of horizontal bars and dashes. The dashes, *yin*, the result of two or three tails, represent receptiveness, femininity, yielding, accepting. The solid lines, *yang*, the result of two or three heads, represent creativity, masculinity, action, initiative. Ultimately, all decisions are a balance between doing and not doing.

There are sixty-four possible combinations. Each of the hexagrams drawn as a result of tossing the coins has a name and is associated with text about a wise person's alternatives, given the import of the hexagram. The introductory chapter in Michael's copy says that the hexagrams and associated texts have been in use for more than three-thousand years, so there are enormous linguistic and cultural differences to be overcome in understanding the "true" meaning of the translations, which vary from one translated edition to another, and there have been several published in English. In his edition, Michael finds the texts so obscure that they can mean almost anything the coin-tosser wants them to mean.

The *I Ching* is a way of understanding change. The hexagrams are not magic, they are a device to focus the mind on a particular dilemma. The more time one takes to frame the question before tossing the coins, the more likely it is that the text will be meaningful.

"But you can consult the *I Ching* as often as you want," says the woman. "It's only scary the first time. What are you afraid of?"

"I'm not sure."

"Maybe you take it too seriously."

"Maybe. Or maybe I don't take it seriously at all; maybe I think it's just nonsense and not worth the time. My name is Michael Berman."

"My name is Patience Monroe."

"Did your parents name you that?" It's a trend he's read about; people are choosing their own names these days as a way to distance themselves from their disapproving parents.

"They did. I am the fifth generation of girls in a long line of Massachusetts Patiences. People call me Patty."

"How did you end up in Guaymas?"

"Off a yacht. From San Diego. I'm on the crew. We just tied up this morning."

"Wow. How long did it take?"

"Four days. We came down along the Baja Peninsula then crossed the Gulf to Guaymas. After we resupply, we're going all the way down to Panama."

"Sounds like fun."

"What about you?"

"We've got a travel trailer. We're heading toward Oaxaca. My wife and daughter are back at the campsite waiting for me."

"Ah," she says.

"So… Can I ask you about the *I Ching*? Have you figured it out? Do you use it?"

"Yes. All the time."

He says, "So you think there's something to it?"

"Absolutely. For me. For now."

She has strong features - high cheekbones, a slightly crooked little nose. Her hair is a dense tangle of short black curls. He imagines her waistline inside the voluminous dress, her navel, a luxurious thatch of black pubic hair. Is she sending signals or hiding them? Her tanned face is impassive, her eyes once again hidden behind the black sunglasses.

"For you, for now," he echoes. "Tell me about now."

Slowly, she raises her arms and looks skyward. Then she faces him, grins like an imp, and says, "That's the stupidest question I've ever heard. You can't be *told* about now. It is your personal now. No one else can explain it. *You* have to be now. You *are* the now."

"No," he says. "Absolutely not true. I am in the world. It is impossible for me to be me alone. Even without people, there is a universe that shapes my attention."

"Ooh," she says.

There is a stillness about her that draws him, a calming that he needs, pulling him in, inviting him closer. Perhaps that's all he's seeking – calm; to be rid of his cursed, incessant thoughts. It would be fine to see her naked, to bury his face in her soft belly, to fill his senses so full of her that she becomes the universe.

"Are you married?" he asks.

She stretches her arm toward him, offering her hand. "Hello, Michael Berman," she says.

Her skin, where their hands touch, is soft and smooth. "Hello, Patty Monroe," he says.

Remus Eats a Lizard

Hannah is missing her Daddy. She wants him to meet Remus. Mommy likes Remus. And she likes Dean, the *Winnebago* man. He's nice. Mommy is talking a blue streak to him, more than to Daddy. Usually, Mommy and Daddy don't talk about anything. When they talk at all, it's to her. But now Mommy is talking, talking, talking. And laughing. It's not often that Mommy laughs.

Dean says to her, "Hannah? Would you like to play fetch with Remus."

"Yes," she says.

"Well then go over there and see if you can find a stick. Not too big, not too small. A nice stick that he can carry back to you, no matter how far you throw it."

"That's a good idea," Mommy says. "I'll watch. See if you can find the perfect stick."

There are sticks on the ground in the mesquite bushes, a lot of them. She runs down the dune with Remus and they go across the bare dirt where the trailer and the *Winnebago* are parked into the sparse edge of the mesquite that dots the plain all the way out to the red cliffs far away. She looks back and sees that Mommy is watching and they wave at each other. It feels nice to be barefoot. Why don't dogs wear shoes? Usually, Mommy doesn't like her to get her feet dirty. Daddy likes to be barefoot, too. "It's just dirt," Daddy says.

Remus is looking, too. He is going from bush to bush, sniffing them, sniffing the ground. She finds a stick and shows it to Remus and he tries to grab it. "No, no, Remus. I have to throw it first," she says, and does, but it doesn't go very far. She must find one that's heavier, so she goes deeper into the mesquite.

The movie set is not far ahead. She has walked to it with Daddy every day. He likes to climb up the back of the tower and look at the ocean while Hannah looks for lizards. There are lizards on every bush. Sometimes they let her get close. She doesn't want to catch one, she just likes to look at them. One of them zips down the trunk of a bush and starts to run, but Remus wants to catch it. And he does! Then he eats it, just like that. He chews it once or twice then swallows it down! Eww!

"Remus," she says. "That's not good for you. It's not nice."

She finds the perfect stick, half as long as her arm and easy to hold. She tosses it underhand, back in the direction of the dune, and it flies over a bush, end over end. Remus grabs it as soon as it touches the ground and brings it back to her, dropping it at her feet.

Mommy, far away now, is waving at her. She's never been this far away from a grownup before. She waves back.

Every time she throws the stick, Remus brings it back. Every time she throws the stick, she walks a few steps farther from the dune where Dean and Mommy are talking, talking, talking.

Usually, she likes to hear what Mommy is saying. Hannah doesn't like to be left out. In Philadelphia, when they are visiting her parents' families, she doesn't like playing with her cousins, she likes sitting with the grownups and listening to what they're saying. Other kids don't like to play with her much anyway. She doesn't know what will happen to her when she starts school. But Remus likes her. Right now, she doesn't care what Dean and Mommy are saying.

Soon, she will be five years old, then she'll be six and go to kindergarten. But she's four, and six is too far away to imagine. She will have a birthday in Mexico soon. January Twentieth is her birthday. It's November now, then December, and then January. Maybe her cousins will come to Mexico for her party. That would be nice.

The Resentment Drawer

Karen and Dean stand watching Hannah and Remus, a little girl and a sleek, black dog. Behind the adults, a warm, placid cove opens to a far horizon. Karen is pleased to see Hannah at play, the child's energy tested by a dog who senses her intentions, and joins her play, wagging his tail.

"I'm starting to worry about Michael," Karen says. "He's been gone for hours."

Dean says, "You can't just drive down the road and find a welder. He may have to travel quite a way to get what he needs. It takes time. How long has he been gone?"

She says, "About three hours, I'd guess. I don't wear a watch."

It's one of Michael's peculiarities - an aversion to timepieces. He looks away from clocks in store windows and steeples. He'd left their wind-up, bedside clock in a cardboard box in Ted and Bea's garage on the morning they departed Los Angeles. She hadn't noticed its absence until after they crossed the border, until after they had stopped at a barren campground a hundred miles south of Tijuana, the night they'd met the Frenchman.

"Where's the clock?" she'd asked.

"We don't need it," he'd said with his usual certainty.

She'd pursed her lips and put her hands on her hips and glared at him. "Are you nuts?" she'd said.

He'd said, "We don't need to know what time it is."

"Speak for yourself," she'd said. "Of course I need to know what fucking time it is. Jesus!"

"Do you? Why?"

"Just because, that's why. Jesus Christ. You should have asked me."

"I want to try living in another kind of time. I thought you understood."

"No. I have no idea whatsoever about what you're talking about. We need to know what time it is."

"If we need to know, we can always find out."

His egocentric decision rankles; another slight she keeps tucked away in the drawer of her resentments.

Now, she says to Dean, "Too long, I think. Do you think he could be in trouble?"

"I doubt it. Does he speak Spanish?"

"Not much. But it doesn't seem to get in his way. Michael talks to everyone, even if they laugh at him. He laughs with them. But he's very polite and respectful, and people answer his questions as if they are his long-lost cousins, and he listens as if he understands. He's very likable."

"What about you?"

"What do you mean? Do I like him?"

"No, I meant do you speak Spanish?"

"Oh," she laughs. "I'm trying. But he's better at it. He had a few years of Latin and a year of Spanish, so he can usually get the gist. But he's way ahead of me, so I let him do the talking." She pauses, assessing her daughter's condition, then says, "I think Hannah's getting tired."

He places his thumb and the middle finger of his massive right hand at the corners of his mouth and whistles, to which Remus responds by spinning around and loping back to the bottom of the sand dune, where he stands, looking up at Dean.

"What?" says Dean. "You lazy dog - get your ass up here." He points to a spot on the sand by his side, and the dog labors up the dune, as if to say, "Aw shucks. Just when I was having fun."

When the dog arrives at his side, Dean grips the back of it's neck, clasping a thickness of muscle and black fur in his powerful grip, and squats in front of the dog, his face inches from the the animal's muzzle. He yanks the dog's head from side to side. "When I call, you come to me. ME! You know better."

The dog tries to look away from the face of his master, but Dean won't allow it. He seems genuinely angry when he gives the dog a final shake before he lets go and says, "Now you SIT right here."

The dog, tongue lolling, message received, sits down exactly where he's supposed to, and watches Hannah climb the dune. To Karen, he seems to be smiling a doggy smile at the sight of the human child, who'd followed him out of the mesquite shrub, climbing up the steep, sandy slope using all fours in imitation of her quadrupedal friend.

"Did you see us Mommy? Were you watching?"

"Of course I was watching," Karen says.

"Did you see me throw the stick?

"I did. It was terrific."

"Remus always brings it back."

"That's why he's called a retriever," says Dean. "He's a Labrador Retriever."

"Oh," says Hannah, and asks, "Does he always brings things back?"

"Usually. It's what retrievers are meant for. Hannah, can you throw a stick overhand?"

"What's that?"

"Come on," says Dean. "I'll show you."

Sideways, he descends to the base of the dune, apparently enjoying his athleticism, as if he's mastered an obstacle course. The child takes long strides to join him in the parking area. Karen allows the folded chair to fall flat on the sand and stands to watch.

Where the hell is Michael? He needs to be here. He treats everything like a joke – nothing is ever any big deal to him. And look where it's landed them. He thinks he can do anything he wants to. No big deal! God, how he pisses her off.

70

Hannah is aiming stones at a mesquite bush, approaching it closer with each wobbly arc, until she stands a few feet away at can't-miss range. Dean has picked a different target, much farther away, and is hurling beelines at the gnarly plant with the powerful grace of a baseball pitcher.

She'd been around athletic young men during her time as a cheerleader, but she sees in Dean something more than a typical letterman's swagger. She likes the way the thin cotton of his tee shirt lays softly on the long muscles of his back. When he stands to observe Hannah's progress, Karen admires his posture; erect, comfortable in the high wooden heels of his cowboy boots.

She carries the chair down to the trailer and stows it in its place in a storage compartment in the back. Every time she has to open the compartment door, she has to first swing the tire out of the way, drawing her attention to the two dents in the rim, reminding her of the incident on the I-5. No big deal, is what Michael says.

Where the hell is he.

The Miramar Hotel

A"re you married?" he repeats.

"No," she says. "Not anymore."

"You are unattached?" he asks.

She takes her time answering him. "Yes, if I want to be," she says.

It is as if a sea-scented bubble has formed around them. The sounds - mild surf lapping against the wall, screaming gulls – are like unfamiliar music. They stand inches apart, leaning into the waist-high wall, watching pelicans and cormorants attack bait fish rising on the surface in brief, shimmering waves. She is giving off heat that he can feel, like a warm breath against his arm.

"Well," he says. "Too bad - I am… attached."

"Yes," she says, and adds, "If you choose to be. Maybe that's what you should ask the *I Ching*."

"I don't think that's the question. The problem isn't the marriage – it's me. I am so restless that it's tough on a wife and child. But I care about them. Their welfare comes first."

"That's one way to look at it," she says. "But you know that the book will give you other ways to see it."

"The point is that it's not just about *me* and how I see things. Everything I do affects my wife and daughter."

73

The Bermans have found a delicate balance that he doesn't care to upset - it wouldn't be fair.

"So, you are a good man. Just my luck," says Patience Monroe.

"Not so fast," he says. "Give me a minute."

The anchovies have moved elsewhere, the surface is calm again, the birds retake position on their perches to groom themselves and await the next swarm, or rise upward to circle the heights above the harbor. Her skin is pink gold. Her black hair is cut short enough that he can see the silken whorls on the back of her neck. Her braless nipples are stiff under the thin fabric of her dress. He turns to face her, and she turns too, so that they are front to front, only a foot apart.

"We're setting sail for Panama tomorrow morning," she says.

You either do something or you don't, you choose either action or inaction – all the rest is bullshit. Action and inaction both have consequences. Either way, he's as likely as not to regret the next hour. There is a pink pastel hotel across the street, *El Miramar*.

"Shall we see if they have a room?" he says, gesturing at the hotel.

"Absolutely," she says.

He puts his arm around her waist and pulls her to him, and they kiss, open-eyed. Her mouth is soft, wet, her lips lightly parted, just enough for her tongue to touch the tip of his.

At the front desk of the hotel, a fastidious man in a starched guayabera hands them a room key after Michael gives him a hundred-and-ten *pesos* and signs the guest register. The key is attached to a disk tag, marked "22," a number that astonishes him, as if the paired digits are destiny, as if the coincidence is a cosmic endorsement of his decision.

There is no elevator, and he follows her up a flight of stairs and a short distance down a hallway to Room 22. He slides the key into the door lock and they enter a clean, simple space with dark wood furnishings and a double bed with a white coverlet. She drops her bag next to a chair, undoes the straps of her sandals, revealing long, elegant feet. She rises and passes him, and, as she does, she catches his eye, and brushes her wrist across the front his blue jeans, signaling that she wants what's hidden there. She stands with her back to him in front of the window, gazing out to the harbor, and spreads her arms to clutch the curtains on either side, but does not draw them closed. She stands there, open-armed, waiting for him.

He undresses, dropping everything he's wearing onto the floor, and sweeps the pile into a corner with his bare foot. He, comes up behind her, and presses the length of his erect penis against her firm, round ass. His hands find her hips and he squeezes his fingers into the soft side of her abdomen as he drops his face onto the curve of her neck to inhale her scent. He opens his mouth to taste her salt, licks her skin lightly, just once.

She pulls the curtains almost together, leaving a narrow gap for a sunbeam to illuminate the room and the man she's invited into her body. She turns to face him, raises her dress, arching backward, pausing momentarily to allow him to look at her breasts, before she tosses the garment onto the pile of his clothes. She hooks her thumbs on the sides of her black panties, slides them down her thighs, then to her ankles, and kicks them off. The stiff nipples and hemispheres of her breasts draw his palms like honeybees to blossoms. She stands and grabs his ass, pulling him close to kiss him again, closes her eyes to loll in the rush of feeling inside her skin. She groans quietly. She pulls away, takes a step back toward the bed, and looks him over; at his saluting penis, at the ripple muscles of his belly, at his flat chest and broad shoulders. Her eyes crinkle and she smiles. "Nice," she says.

"You too," he says. "Wow."

She turns and crawls onto the bed, leaving a space for him. He joins her and they embrace, belly to belly. He needs to see her, to inhale her with his eyes, to feast on the sight of her. He rises on his knees, puts one hand on her near thigh and the other on a breast. Her pubic hair is dense, alive, dark, and human. She raises her arms and

76

wriggles with pleasure, arches her back off the coverlet. The dark tufts of her armpits complete her perfection.

She drops her arms and turns her attention to his dick, and slowly slides fingers along it to his swollen glans, which she does not touch, then back to the root, then upward again, her fingers tighter. Then she opens her hand and puts her fingers around his penis and squeezes, measuring it, imagining what it will feel like clutched in her vagina. She lets go of him and looks into his face. "Oh," she says, and moans, her eyes half-closed.

He puts his face on her belly and rubs it with his cheek. He presses his lips to her side, into the deep curve above her hip, and trails kisses along her ribcage, lingering where her breast swells, filling his nostrils with her scent - earth and ocean. Then he rises, spreads her thighs apart, and kneels before her. He bends and puts his nose into her thatch, and nuzzles her, and kisses her, searching for her clitoris, and he finds it, the small engorged center of her. He falls onto his belly and licks her nub, his arms under her thighs, and his hands on her hips to keep her thrashing body still. He circles her clitoris with his wet tongue, pressing his face hard, applying pressure that hints of pounding thrusts.

He rises and looks at her face and she returns his gaze, "Okay, okay," she says. "Now!" She puts her hands on her knees and spreads herself wider, fully open. He plants his hands on the mattress at her sides. She reaches for his head and pulls his face to hers, kisses him, excited by the blended scents and juices on his face. He pulls up from her. She raises her head from the pillow and looks down the length of their bodies, reaches for his penis with both hands, and guides it to her vagina. But he resists at the last moment, halting at the entrance. Then, carefully, he slides between the lips of her vulva, barely penetrating her, halting there, fearful that if he goes too far too soon he'll come and it will be over.

She opens her eyes wide. "More," she says. "More!"

He leans down, kisses her eager mouth, slides in all the way, stops, pushes his pubic bone hard against hers, and waits a long moment, savoring the intimacy. "Oh," she says. "Oh, oh."

He pulls partway out. He looks down and sees her belly clench, feels her spasm around his dick. "Oh," she says. "Please." She digs her nails into his back. He thrusts slowly in - then pulls slowly out, then again, and again, each micro-inch a different pleasure - then faster, then faster. She clings to him with arms and she plants her feet on the mattress for leverage, and he goes faster; her moans become stifled shouts; her head back, her neck exposed, her mouth open. They move together - together together together together together together. Her rhythm matches his, synchronous, unconscious.

Now... Now... He comes! Hugely, thoughts obliterated, words banished, sensation radiating from his penis to his every nerve and muscle, from his soles to his scalp, suffusing him, saturating him, overwhelming him, as he empties into a woman.

Spent, mindless - he slides out of her and falls onto his back. She rolls onto her side and puts an arm across his chest.

Michael lies in bed with Patience Monroe, a humming, naked woman stranger with whom he's just had the greatest sex of his life. She is a calm landscape of curves, softness, and contentment. A ceiling fan is cooling their wet parts. She lies on her back, with her eyes closed, smiling. He is nowhere, everywhere. He is not then, not when, he is now. He is.

But he cannot stay. He must return to Hannah and Karen at the trailer. He's been gone too long.

He imagines himself on a sailboat on a sunlit sea. He could leave for Panama in the morning.

He leaves the bed and goes into the bathroom and cleans himself, washing away the scents of semen and of a woman. Karen would be wounded by the knowledge, and he doesn't want to hurt her.

He will not mention it. He will hold this moment for himself. His afternoon with Patience means something significant and he needs time to understand it. He will behave as if fucking with Patience never happened.

She sits up with her back to the headboard and watches him pick his clothes off the floor and put them on. "That was wonderful," she says.

Words. He does not want to hear words. Words get in the way.

"Shush," he says. With his pants safely on, he returns to the bed, straddles the woman, and stares at her face. And she stares back, trying to read him as well, and they each see curiosity and amazement in the other's face. Their smiles broaden to grins.

"I have to go," he says.

"Yes," she says.

"Do you think we'll meet again?"

"Yes, if we choose to," she says. "I could find you if I want to. In Oaxaca."

"And you'll be in Panama. That's not so far. Do you want to?" he asks.

"Do you?"

"Where do you live? When you're not on a boat?"

"San Diego. And you? When you're not in a trailer?"

"I don't know. Wherever I park."

"It's been great," she says.

"Yes," he says.

Simultaneous Orgasm

Well," says Dean, "You've got everything you need? I mean, if you need a lift to town to get groceries, or anything like that, I can drive you."

"Nice to know," Karen says. "But we're in good shape. We shopped yesterday, so the fridge is full, and so's the propane tank, and we brought back ten gallons of good water and topped off our tank. Thanks for the offer, but we're good for awhile. And you shouldn't be driving that big thing around as if it's just a car. It must cost a fortune to run it."

"It costs somebody, but not me. I'm just the truck driver."

"Is that what you did in Vietnam? Drive a truck?"

"Kind of," he says. "We used helicopters more than trucks. The roads were too dangerous."

"So you were a helicopter pilot?"

"Still am, I guess. Got a helicopter?"

She laughs. "We keep it in the trunk."

"Cool," he says, smiling.

Michael doesn't laugh at what she thinks is funny, not that she finds much to laugh about. But now, the helicopter pilot finds her amusing. How nice. She's been so lonesome. She's left her friends in Philadelphia, the women of her age with children. She hasn't had anyone to talk to in months.

"I've got to go feed the dog," he says. "I'll see you later."

"Can I watch?" says Hannah.

"It's up to your Mom," Dean says.

"I'd love to see inside the *Winnebago*," Karen says. "Can I come, too?"

"Why not? Don't mind the mess."

The *Winnebago* is parked thirty yards from the trailer, at the same angle, facing south, the doors of both facing west, opening to the dune. The arvee is three times longer and a foot higher than their utilitarian box on wheels. The dog, as if he understands that he's about to be fed, takes off for the *Winnebago*, with Hannah close behind him. Dean opens the door, tells the dog to stay outside, and ushers Karen and Hannah inside.

The walls are paneled in rich-grained mahogany. The kitchen has a full-sized, stainless steel oven, refrigerator, and sink. The upholstery is black leather and green fabric. The long, narrow sconces mounted to the paneling have frosted glass shades. The floor is carpeted. The windows are framed by forest green curtains with a silken sheen.

Dean hangs his hat on a brass hook, removes a can of dog food from a capacious larder, opens it, spoons the mess into a heavy plastic bowl, carries it back to the outside, and places it on the ground near the door where the dog is waiting. Hannah goes outside to watch, leaving Dean and Karen alone in the trailer.

"Can I look at your bathroom?" Karen asks.

"Sure," says Dean. "Don't mind the mess."

In the Bermans' trailer, there's a a tiny sink under a tiny mirrored medicine cabinet opposite a plastic toilet. The *Winnebago's* full-sized bathroom fixtures are pink porcelain. There's a stall shower and enough counter space to lay out cosmetics and a hair dryer.

"Wow. A shower," Karen says. "I wish we had a shower. We use the ones at the campgrounds. This is *so* nice."

"Well, it works. You're welcome to use it."

"Really? We might take you up on that."

"Be my guest," says Dean. "Just come on over and I'll get out of the way. It's not a problem."

She checks on her daughter. Hannah is sitting on the ground next to Remus, who, satisfied by his meal, has laid his head on his forepaws in preparation for a snooze. He lifts his head when Karen opens the door.

Karen says, "How you doing, kiddo?"

"I'm okay. Remus liked his supper."

"Why don't you stay with him and keep him company? You can get Barbie."

"Okay."

"Or you could practice throwing overhand. I think you're getting good at it."

"Okay," says Hannah. "I'll get Barbie and I'll show her how I throw."

When Karen closes the door, she depresses the button in the handle, locking it. Dean is watching her. She meets his eyes. "Where do you sleep?" she asks.

He gives her a long look and points to a closed mahogany door that conceals the back third of the *Winnebago's* interior space. "Have a look. Don't mind the mess." He stands aside to let her pass. She steps to the door and turns the handle. He stands behind her as she surveys the space, the tang of his sweat enveloping her like a delicious fog.

There is no mess other than on the bedside table - a book and a glass ashtray with a half a joint in it. The double bed is made up with military precision - no blanket, a top sheet pulled taut, two pillows.

She is turned-on in a new way. With Michael, she responds to his touch, if at all. With Dean, she is aroused by the sight of him, by his presence. The nearer he is, the stronger she feels the need. She is imagining sex before it happens. It is desire - new and delicious. For the first time in her life, she wants to make it happen, to be the taker, to pull a man into her, to fuck this muscular cowboy until he explodes inside her. She's on The Pill, so there will be no pregnancy; any other consequences seem trivial.

She turns around to see him and her need swells as she looks at his hard body. He is looking at her, leaning slightly forward. She smiles at the excitement she sees in his eyes. He wants her! She is the object of his desire! Then the space between them disappears as they step toward each other. Looking at her face, he places his big hands on her shoulders.

She closes her eyes and feels his arms fold around her, and she leans into the embrace, her face against his chest, hears the throbbing beat of his heart, wraps her arms around his waist, and hugs him tightly. She feels his cock pressing into her belly, and she tilts her hips into him.

He's so tall. She looks up to be kissed, and he obliges. His lips are full, dry, and hot. She opens her mouth and licks them wet. He groans, deep in his throat, and the sound affects her as if he'd turned up a flame. Her knees bend, and she is soft all over, her joints melted by the hot juice of need.

He holds her tighter, and lifts her off the ground, dragging her up the front of his body, and he kisses her with parted lips, and she thrusts her tongue to fill his mouth. His cock is large and hard inside his jeans. She raises her knees, clasps his hips, and pushes her pussy down on his bulging cock. He growls low and deep in his throat

She frees herself and stands in front of him. She reaches down and presses her palm against his cock, feeling its girth and length. She uses both hands and undoes his belt buckle, then the brass button at the top of his fly, and pulls the zipper down. But he is still not free, and she grabs the tops of his shorts and jeans with both hands and pulls them down to his thighs, releasing his big, stiff cock.

She gulps as saliva fills her mouth. She touches his amazing cock, grasps it, and looks at his face. He takes the blouse off her shoulders and lets it drop to the floor. Then he pulls the straps of her bathing suit down over her arms and pulls the black rayon down over her hips, then tugs further, exposing her navel. He kneels and pulls her into his face, rubbing her breasts with his soft-stubbled cheeks. She cradles his head and he sucks one nipple, gently, then the other, harder.

They undress. She wriggles out of the bathing suit and stands before him, watching him, pleased at the approval she sees in his eyes. He sits on the edge of the bed, yanks his boots off, then his socks. As she watches him take off his shorts and jeans, she reaches down to her pussy and puts her fingers to the juice – she has so much - and rubs it over her swollen clitoris.

He pulls his tee shirt over his head. His arms and face are a ruddy tan, the rest of him is ivory-toned, thick and smooth. Sitting on the edge of the bed, he opens his arms, inviting her to join him.

She steps to the bed and puts her hands on his shoulders as she straddles him. He falls back and she drops onto him, reaches his cock with a hand and holds it to her clit, then she rubs his cock with her wet pussy, grinding, wriggling. He reaches down and touches her pussy with busy fingers. She leans forward, and crawls up the bed. He shimmies up to the pillow. Then she raises up, stretching her torso with her hands behind her head, so that he can look at her. Then he reaches around and clutches her buttocks, pulling her off balance so that she must drop onto her hands. Then he reaches her juicy lips with his fingers and parts them. She raises up once more, reaches down, takes hold of his moistened cock, aims it, puts her pussy lips around it, and eases down sliding wriggling shimmying to fill herself with his cock.

He arches his back, and pulls her by the ass so that she is on all fours with her her tits over his face, and he licks a nipple. Slowly, he pulls out, then in again, and she pushes hard, to feel his pelvic bone on her clitoris, but he's stronger, and pulls away again, then he *slams* her, *and she comes*. Her hands are beside his head, her vagina parallel to the mattress, and she joins his game now moving with him, now against him, rocking back and forth in time with his slow thrusts, again and again, *and she comes,* and he speeds up, digging his fingers into her ass, *and she comes* as he clutches, and she matches him, then he goes faster than she can keep up, and she holds still as he fucks her *and she comes* and he fucks her and fucks her harder and faster fucking faster faster faster and she pushes back to slow him, pleading with whimpers for him to erupt now now now now NOW.

He comes, filling her completely, his cock pulsing as the semen pumps through it, bathing her pussy with white juice gushers again and again and again *and SHE COMES and she comes* and she comes.

PART TWO

Destiny

Going in the opposite direction, with the sun lower, the road from Guaymas to the ranchero seems unfamiliar. He slows as he passes Pete's repair shop, but sees no one about to wave at, and speeds up. Then, enjoying the nimbleness of the car without it's burden, he goes as fast as the straight road will allow, past farm buildings, cactus, and Joshua trees. The dirt road into Catch 22 is hard to spot from the highway, and he overshoots it.

He could keep going. He could.

After a hundred yards of indecision, he makes a U-turn and steers his car into the side road, drives along its curves between rocky hillsides for a mile-and-a-half of ruts and potholes. When he emerges onto the narrow plain of mesquite behind the beach, he sees the movie set, and a quarter mile farther off, the sand dune, their trailer, and a huge arvee. He is apprehensive about how he will behave with Karen.

He parks the car with the hitch ball a few feet from the trailer's socket, ready for a quick getaway. Hannah runs into his arms as soon as he closes the car door.

"Daddy. Guess what?" She is buoyant, pleased with herself.

"What? Tell me… what?"

"There's a dog here! And he likes to play with me. Remus is his name. He's a Labrador Retriever. He brings everything back."

"Wow," he says. "That's terrific."

"And he swims with me. And we had a shower. In the *Winnebago.*"

He looks to Karen, a few feet away. "Really? A shower?"

"Yeah," says Karen. "The owner offered. So how'd you do? Did you get it fixed?"

He puts Hannah down. "I did. It's as good as new. Better than. I found a shop with a welder and he fixed it right away. No problem. I had them put extra welds on it so it doesn't happen again."

"You must be starving."

"No," he says, "I went into Guaymas and ate at an outdoor restaurant."

"Oh no! You didn't!"

"I did. I was hungry. Don't worry, everything was cooked to death. I'll be all right."

"While we were back here, alone, you went and had lunch. Nice."

"It was, actually," he says. "Exceptional."

"So what's Guaymas like?"

"There's nothing much there. You won't be missing anything if we pass it by."

"What's there?"

"A church, a market square. A lot of poor houses and a little waterfront. That's where I ate. Carnitas – that's grilled meat in tortillas."

"I hope it was safe."

"Me, too," he says. "So who are the people in the *Winnebago*?"

"His name is Dean," says Hannah.

"And?"

"And Remus," Hannah says.

"That's the dog. Who else? Any kids?" he asks

"No," says Karen. "Just this guy named Dean and his dog."

"You're hair looks different," he says.

" I used a blow dryer. In Dean's bathroom."

"Oh," he says. "You look nice."

"So you're not hungry? You said you'd be back for supper, so we waited."

"I can eat," he says. "Lunch was awhile ago. So who's this guy in the *Winnebago*?"

"He's a cowboy," Hannah says.

"You mean with a hat and a horse and all that?"

"No horse," answers the little girl, "But he is a cow-boy, no doubt about it."

"Well, I can't wait to meet him," Michael says.

Supper is spaghetti and meat sauce from a jar, both boiled to sterility. After they eat, as they're cleaning up, he says he feels like taking a walk. "Let's go out onto the rocks and watch the sunset."

"No," says Karen. "We've had enough of the outdoors for one day. Hannah played with that dog until she was ready to drop. She's exhausted. Me too. I think maybe I had too much sun."

"You do look a little pink," he says. "So. All right then, I'll go by myself."

He takes a sweatshirt from a compartment above the window in back. He says. "Are you sure you don't want to come?"

She blinks. "Not right now," she says.

He is pleased with the way his homecoming has worked out, his earlier apprehension having been allayed by the ease with which he's hidden his transgression. Karen seems perfectly normal, and he has no trouble omitting the fucking of Patience from his narrative of the day's events. It's over. The moment has passed, an extraordinary moment to be sure, but just another moment, this one bigger and brighter than any he had ever before experienced, but just a moment nonetheless. The path continues, the moments never stop.

Weather is moving in from the sea, the horizon is indistinct, obscured by clouds blowing toward land, the mist softening the sun disk to a bright blur. This is his tenth sunset on the promontory at Catch 22, and he loves the view as much as he did that first evening.

It means something. *She* means something. The woman, Patience Monroe, Patty from San Diego, the incredible woman, was some kind of messenger. But what's the message? And the number business is so weird, the coincidence of twenty-twos. And two times one-ten, the cost of the room, is two-twenty. And what does the *I Ching*, have to do with it? It had been the reason he and Patience had connected. Could it be? Is there some kind of destiny working here? He doesn't believe in destiny. Things happen for rational reasons or by accident, but not because some Guiding Hand arranges them to send messages to mortals. But... Still...

The outcropping on which he stands is mostly raw rock with a few brave cactus, tufts of sea grass, and a scatter of wildflowers. It extends some distance into the sea from the beach, a long walk that requires attention to the footing. Birds roost on boulders and the weathered pillars where the waves strike. The highest flyers, the Frigate Birds, with streaming tails and long wings, can rest in the updrafts as they wait. They amaze him.

The dog, he's guessing it's Remus, appears atop the dune before his master. Michael notices them immediately, appearing like actors on a stage lit by the setting sun, standing side by side, scanning the panorama. The cowboy notices him, raises his arm in a greeting, then leads the dog down onto the perfect beach where they make footprints on the wave-smoothed sand, heading for the promontory.

Michael is curious about this stranger who travels alone in a conveyance that's as big as a school bus. He does not like the excess of motor homes, and he is mistrustful of people who drive them, people who bring motorcycles and trail bikes and outboard motors to the quiet places, people who run their big smelly engines to cool themselves as they play with their gadgets.

He watches the man in the cowboy hat approach. He's younger than most arvee owners, who tend to be retired *gringos* enjoying the favorable rate of exchange. This guy is wearing cowboy boots, is fit, athletic, big. But what's with the hat? Michael wears leather sandals, faded jeans and work shirts with sleeves rolled to his elbows.

"Hey," says the cowboy, extending his hand. "You must be Michael. I'm Dean Scanlon," They shake. Dean's grip is firm, like his.

"This is an incredible place," says Dean.

"Yes it is," says Michael.

In campground etiquette, talk of roads and vehicles is always appropriate, a way of making conversation with temporary neighbors. "That's an awful big rig," Michael says, "How'd it do on the road in?"

"Just fine. The suspension can handle roads like this. I just had to come in slow."

"How'd you find out about this place?"

"I have a map. The guy I'm delivering the *Winnebago* to mapped out the whole trip down from West Texas."

"West Texas? Is that where you're from?"

"Midland, way out in the sagebrush. Your wife tells me you've been here over a week."

"You'll have the place to yourself tomorrow morning. We'll be leaving first thing."

"She told me you guys are heading for Oaxaca. Me too."

"Really? How about that. What's it like?"

"I've never been there," says Dean.

"Have you been to Mexico before?"

"Only just up around the border, once or twice, for a few days. But listen, I want to pay for the space. There's some guy named Fernando who I have to see?"

"Don't worry, he'll be around."

Fernando is one of the reasons Michael is leaving. He had been prepared for Fernando's visit on the second night, more than willing to provide the man with cash in exchange for the privilege of camping at Catch-22. But

Fernando had eschewed money for beer and Michael's company. He'd shown up every night. On the second night, he'd built a campfire on the dune. That night, and every night thereafter, the two new friends sat and enjoyed Michael's beer and cigarettes. For Michael, the regular campfires were tutorials in conversational Spanish. For Fernando, they were free beer and cigarettes.

But the evenings had begun to seem like an obligation, particularly after last night. Fernando had insisted that Michael bring him back a bottle of vodka the next time he went to buy groceries. Last night, he'd watched as Fernando swigged from the bottle, sang off-key Mexican love songs, and fell asleep on the sand before the fire went out. This morning, determined to leave, he'd discovered the broken hitch.

"How much do you pay him?" Dean asks.

"I can't say. He took a shine to us and never asked us for money. But anyone else who's come in here has had to pay. Since we've been here, there have been a couple of other campers, but they only stayed for one night. Maybe Fernando chased them off. You'd best be nice to him."

"And what time does he come by?"

"About now. If you want to make a deal, you probably ought to be with your rig. Offer him a beer."

Sins of Omission

Karen hurries their shower, soaping and rinsing Hannah quickly, anxious to be outside before Michael returns. Something magical has happened. Truly… Magic. Sex with Dean had been a revelation. There had been a certainty to it from the moment she'd seen him step onto the bare dirt, as if he had been sent to the dune specifically for her. She has never felt this way, this powerfully, before. And she doesn't feel shame, as she had wanted it, had begged for it. Lust, pure and simple, and it had been fantastic.

They make it back to their trailer in time for her to set the pans on the stove and prepare a meal for Hannah and Michael. Hannah looks cute, with her hair poofed out by the electric dryer.

It had been so sudden, like a bolt from the beyond. It had just happened.

She and Hannah watch Michael park, and Hannah runs to greet him.

She feels whole, as if jangling parts of her have been pulled to her center.

Michael seems happy, somehow pleased with himself, wearing that smile that aggravates her so. But he's a happy guy. Except for her, everything seems to make him happy. He marvels at the little and the big, at the beautiful and the ugly. She never knows what will next capture his attention, zigzagging all the time as he does, hopping from one subject to another, following weird connections inside his nonstop head. He is an enthusiast who reaches out, oblivious of risk. She deals with consequences, not causes. He makes trouble, she resolves it. That's how it is. There's too much at stake to do otherwise.

And, watching the child, she is reminded that Hannah does love her Daddy, thriving on his enthusiasm and his affection. They have a rapport that warms her heart. How the hell could she have done what she did? My God! What has she done?

How can she pretend that she's not a different person, as if what happened in Dean's bed had not changed her. He says that I look "a little pink." Oh yes.

She'll see how it goes. She'll act as if nothing has happened. She will do nothing and wait. And Dean is traveling on the same roads, going to the same place. It could happen again.

Michael goes out for a walk, and she sees to Hannah's bedtime. She loves reading to Hannah, enlivening the text with exaggerated emotion and facial expressions. Hannah follows along as Karen runs her fingertip under the text, teaching the letters and the words. Hannah's only four and is already reading simple books on her own. Precious child.

Michael wants them to have another baby, but she doesn't feel it's the right time, not with so much uncertainty about their future. It takes so much to raise one child, it would be so much more difficult with two, especially if Michael is not there to help. No. This is no time to get pregnant. It would be nice for Hannah to have a sibling, true, but the little girl seems to be getting along just fine as an only child. Karen likes her relationship with her darling daughter, it's enough for both of them.

The prospect of a sibling for Hannah is a hold she has over Michael. She hasn't said she's done having children, only that she's done for the time being, holding out hope, a prospect that helps to keep Michael in the marriage. He thinks it's important to take some of the pressure off the little girl, to divert her parents' overweening attentions away from its focus on her alone by adding a baby brother or sister to their family. Hannah would become accustomed to sharing and to compromise, important life strategies. But Hannah is fine, just fine, a wonderful little girl. His concerns about their daughter are unwarranted. She had been an only child herself, and there's nothing wrong with her, goddammit.

And this is a matter that she can control, thanks to The Pill. Too bad if Michael doesn't like it. He's turned their life upside down and she has hung on through all of his craziness. Considering all she's had to put up with, all the times he has had his way and forced her to deal with it, it's only fair that she hold onto the trump card. Another pregnancy is a matter that she can decide, and his opinion be damned. She is in charge of her body, not him. Childbirth is no picnic, buster.

If she does decide to get pregnant, she would have to believe in the future of their marriage. If she were to change her mind, it would be the same as saying she's satisfied with the way things are between her and Michael, and that's certainly not so. Maintaining the walls of amicable avoidance between them is hard work, tolerable, but devoid of joy. Until this afternoon, she'd felt undesirable, withered by Michael's disappointment. Now she knows she has worth as a woman - she can be complete without him.

He returns from his outing on the promontory just after Hannah is safely up in her bunk above the table, guardrail up, all blankets and cuddly toys appropriately arranged. She is asleep, thumb near her mouth, her other hand near a Barbie Doll.

"Let's go outside," he whispers.

"I don't feel real great," she says. "I was up on the dune and I fell asleep. I got way too much sun."

"I talked to Dean," he says.

"Oh? And?"

"He has another idea about the roads to Oaxaca. We might be changing our plans."

"Okay," she says wearily, "I guess I've got to hear about it."

He leads her through the trailer door onto the beaten dirt behind the dune. It's dark out.

Fernando is in an officious mood. The Mexican caretaker is telling Dean that he cannot park his *Winnebago* at Catch-22. "*Porque es mas grande,*" he says, speaking slowly, so that the *gringo* understands. Too big.

Fernando is opening a negotiation, but Dean takes it another way. "Too big for what? For who?" he says. Beside him, the dog Remus is watchful.

The weary old horse, restless at the end of the bridle in Fernando's hand, wants to be away from the dog. Fernando tightens his grip, gives a yank, and says, "*No se permite. Es la regla.*"

Michael intervenes, says, "Que tal, Fernando."

"*Ah, Miguel. Todavia estas aqui. Por que?*" says Fernando, surprised that the Bermans are still there.

"Mi coche tiene un problema. Hoy, in Guaymas, para las reparaciones. Adios mañana." He thinks he's saying that he went to Guaymas to fix a problem with his car, and that he's leaving tomorrow.

And so he's drawn into a negotiation between Dean and Fernando. They discuss the matter over three bottles of Dean's beer as Karen looks on. Dean agrees to leave in the morning, and he hands Fernando twenty *pesos* for his troubles. Fernando goes away, happy to have collected enough money for a bottle of vodka.

"Do you think he'll let me stay after tomorrow?" Dean asks.

"It depends on whether he thinks twenty *pesos* a night is fair. But he's got a point; that's a big goddamned rig," says Michael.

"Well, I was only going to stay here two nights, anyways. So I'll get to Culiacan a day early. That's not a problem."

"You're going to Culiacan? What's there?" Michael asks. He has studied the map showing the city of Culiacan about three-hundred miles South of Guaymas. He had intended it as their next destination, as it has a listed campground recommended by the *Triple-A*. Had he not had a broken hitch, they would be there right now.

"Actually, I haven't." Dean says. "But I've got to be there. Is that where you're heading."

"It is," says Michael. "Culiacan, then Mazatlan, Guadalajara, and Mexico City. It should only take a day to drive from Mexico City to Oaxaca."

"Same as me," says Dean. "That's the same route that I'm taking."

"Hannah will be delighted," says Karen. "She just loves Remus."

Dean reaches into his pocket and removes a metal cigarette case, from which he extracts a nicely rolled joint, and fires it up with a *Zippo* lighter. He tokes and, in a choked voice, says, "Want some?"

"Well, thanks," says Michael. In fact, he's been looking to score some pot; he's been told that it is readily available in Mexico. Their meager supply is at the bottom of a baggy concealed in the trailer's ceiling. He takes one of Dean's joints and lights it up from the Zippo, its wavering flame bright in the darkness. He inhales a lungful and hands it to Karen, who does the same. They've been smokers since graduate school, scoring an ounce once or twice every year.

They talk about the scenery. Dean asks about places for gas and food. They talk about the news, about Watergate, about the peace negotiations taking place in Paris, and agree that the war cannot end soon enough, that Nixon is as guilty as sin. They talk about music, and discover a mutual fondness for acid rock, and, of course, *The Beatles*.

"Mostly, I like classical music," Michael says.

"I never got into it," says Dean.

So, having established some interests in common, they agree to travel together in the morning. If they keep a different pace, they will separate and look for each other at the campground on the outskirts of Culiacan tomorrow evening.

In bed together, Karen whispers that she's not feeling well. Michael, thinking about Patience Monroe, does not protest.

The Audition

Karen drops off as Michael re-reads the introductory chapters of the *I Ching* by the battery powered light on his side of the headboard. He switches off the light after half an hour, but cannot sleep, cannot quiet the turmoil.

The amazing interlude with Patience might be a bizarre coincidence of no greater import than a random collision. Fucking is fucking; it is what it is. The message may simply be that life is beautiful, occasionally spectacular. One simply puts one foot in front of the other and enjoys the scenery. But where is the path? And isn't that what *The Tao* means – *The Path*?

He's not sure why he doesn't want to toss the damned coins and be done with it. Part of it is because he doesn't take advice easily; he dislikes the idea that some old book can influence his choices. Too, the very notion of divination defies rationalism, and he is a rational man. And yet, he is drawn to the book. Patience Monroe had been reading from it at another table, at the same improbable place at the same improbable time. How can that not be destiny at work?

If destiny is truly operating, then the answers in the *I Ching* are a form of truth, and the consequence of throwing the coins is therefore frightening. Really? TRUTH?

From an ancient Chinese book? If he doesn't throw the coins, it means he doesn't buy the whole deal. He believes that his destiny will be shaped by his choices and he doesn't want some old conjurer's book to fog his mind.

And then there's the question of the question. He wants to be a writer, he thinks. But how should he ask the question? Should I? Could I? Will I? And what if the answer is no, no, no. Then what? Of all the things he wants to know, the question of whether he will be what he wants to be is the question he's most afraid to ask – but why ask anything else?

When he'd been a kid, his big brother had told him a golden rule, "You either do it or you don't, whatever it is," Steve had said. "It's not what you say, it's what you do. All the rest is bullshit." Okay. That had seemed true. That was his credo, wasn't it? He'd not whined about his life, he'd done something about it. Lying next to his sleeping wife, he recalls declaring as much at a crucial moment, during an encounter when he probably should have said something else. "Just do it," he'd said. That had been a strange day, too.

Staying in Ted and Bea Silver's house after arriving in California, they'd been tourists: Hollywood Boulevard, Watts Tower, the Tar Pits, *Disneyland*, Beverly Hills, Topanga Canyon. In the mornings, after the Silvers left for work, before setting out with Karen and Hannah to see the sights, Michael had scanned the want-ads in *The Los Angeles Times*, considering the sprawling city as a potential home, the place where he'd find a job, a place where they might settle down. Perhaps the question was not "What to do?" as much as it was "Where to be?"

He'd declared his brother's philosophy as his own a few days after they had arrived in California. He'd blurted it out as if he believed it. He'd been reading *The Times*, found an announcement for a quiz show audition, and decided to go for it. Karen and Hannah were happy for a break from touring and pleased to cool out in front of the Silvers' television and a pile of magazines.

"Wish me luck!" he'd said in the doorway.

"Bye Daddy," said Hannah, enjoying *Sesame Street* in color.

"Good luck," said Karen from the couch. He had grown accustomed to the neutrality of Karen's tone. As is the way in fragile marriages, he was as even-toned as she. "I'll try not to get lost," he'd said, and headed off to find the television studio.

Karen, asleep beside him, is dreaming, muttering. What does she dream? Awake, she is passively angry at him for disrupting their lives, stifling resentment, pretending that she does not worry about the future. He does not blame her; it *is* all his doing.

The television studio had been in a big room with a dozen rows of banked seats, a host's podium, and scenery flats in neutral colors. Even though he'd gotten there a half-hour early, most of the seats were filled by the time he'd arrived. Exactly on time, as specified in the ad, a woman stepped to the podium. She was unglamorous and harassed, like any lady in her forties he might see in a supermarket aisle.

"I'm a producer on this show - Theresa Delahunt. Call me Theresa. Thank you all for coming today. We are trying to select a few lucky people. But, let me say, and I hope you're paying attention, if you have any other place at all to be at today, you might be better off there. Most of you, maybe even all of you, will be told to go home after the first interview. But we'll be needing all of you to stay here until we finish the first round, which is going to take at least a couple of hours. Don't take it personally, but most of you are not what we're looking for, so be ready to be disappointed. Okay? Nobody should get their hopes up. Okay? So if you want to leave, do it now."

Apparently, nobody had any better place to be. Clipboards with forms like employment applications were passed out, completed, and returned. One by one, the candidates were called for interviews somewhere behind the scenery flats. Michael was one of the last to be summoned.

He was told to take a seat with a stage light beaming onto it. Opposite, behind a desk and stacks of the completed forms, sat Theresa Delahunt. "Who is Michael Berman?" she'd asked.

"I'm a teacher. From Philadelphia. Or was. I'm out here in California, checking it out, kind of looking around."

"So, you're one of those dropouts?" She'd asked, a weary woman accustomed to disappointment.

He'd smiled and shrugged.

"So, what do you think of LA?"

"There's a lot of traffic. Nice houses. Even your slums have nice houses. The weather's great. I hear it's like this most of the time, right?"

The atmosphere is different in the arid West; the shapes of things sharper to his eye in the dry air. In southeastern Pennsylvania, even with Fall approaching, the world is lush and green with trees and weeds crowding every untended space. LA had seemed the reverse; the untended areas brownish and brittle, and only the watered and managed places green and lush. Absent the moisture and thawing cycles that weather buildings on the East Coast, Southern California houses, even if they are decades old, seemed new to him. In the sprawling neighborhoods, even Watts, buildings seem suburban-fine, like the *Plasticville* models he and his brother had snapped together and arranged around their electric train set. To him, there is a toy-like aspect to the whole of Los Angeles, a city purpose-built in the Automobile and Airplane Age, so different from the warren of narrow Philadelphia streets where he'd grown up. Philadelphia had been built for horse-drawn wagons, LA for cars and trucks.

"Pretty much," Teresa Delahunt had replied, clearly disinterested in a conversation about the weather in Southern California. "So, what kind of teacher are you?"

"Speech. How to make speeches."

"That sounds interesting."

"I suppose. You have to listen to the students, though, over and over. Lots of sophomore speeches."

"Oh."

He had been boring her. Perhaps he was not upbeat enough, or maybe he was too square.

She glanced down at her clipboard. "You're from Philadelphia. Did you ever go to *Bandstand?* Dick Clark's *Bandstand* show? You know, where everybody danced? I loved that show."

Michael is an awkward dancer. "No. Not my thing."

"So, what *is* your thing?"

That had been his chance to be hip, but nothing had come to mind.

Seeing his vacant expression, she'd offered another prompt. "So, you know, like what's your philosophy of life?"

That was when he remembered Steve's philosophy - that you either did something or you didn't do it, that all the rest is bullshit. "Just do it," Michael had answered.

The producer frowned. "That's it?"

"Well…" he'd said. Funny, when it had mattered, he hadn't been able think of anything to say. "Right now, I guess so… Just do it."

"Do what?"

"Whatever it is that you need to do. Don't talk about it. Just do it."

"Okay. Thank you," the producer had said, and moved on to the next candidate.

That moment, in retrospect, seems to have been destined. But then, everything seems like destiny in retrospect.

At last, he falls asleep.

A Little Advice

On the road to Culiacan, sitting next to Michael, Karen keeps an eye on the wing mirror mounted to the Dodge's passenger-side fender. Behind them, Dean follows in his *Winnebago*. She checks frequently, barely noticing the dull, sunlit landscape and the scattered, shabby towns. Occasionally, the hilly terrain on her right opens up, affording glimpses of the Sea of Cortez. But the sea views don't impress her, they don't even register on her consciousness.

Hannah is okay, strapped-in on the back seat, wrapping different-colored ribbons around her Barbie Dolls.

Michael, hands on the wheel, watching the road, seems calmer than usual this morning.

Bea Silver had said something when they'd been at her house in Los Angeles. "Ducks in a row," is how Bea had put the matter. She'd come home for a quick lunch between showing houses, and they had been together in the kitchen, with Hannah watching TV in the living room.

Bea looks like a fashion model: tall, rail-thin, and pretty. The Silvers are attractive people, the kind who turn heads in Philadelphia, but are closer to the norm in Los Angeles. She had been getting jobs as a catalog model when she'd met Ted Silver at UCLA, Now, she is a real estate agent. That day in the kitchen had been the first time that Karen and Bea had a chance to talk alone, woman to woman, since the Bermans had arrived.

Bea said, "I'm putting the kettle on. Do you want a cup of tea? Where's Michael?"

"Thanks. He went to a quiz show audition."

"Well, good luck with that."

"He's pretty smart. He thinks he has a good chance."

"So," said Beatrice, "What's the story?"

"The story? We're going to Mexico. We'll see."

"I mean with you and Michael. How's it going?"

"It's as good as it can be. Fine," she'd said. "We're fine… mostly. He's all excited about the trip."

"And you?"

"It should be fun. Michael thinks we have enough money saved to stay down there for months, maybe even a year. They say the cost of living is so much lower than it is in The States."

"But the two of you? I mean, I thought you'd have at least one more baby by now."

"Well, the timing's not very good, is it?"

"What about Michael? Does he want more children?"

"He says so. But he says a lot of things and then changes his mind. I don't think I want to bring another child into the marriage right now. It was all I could do to keep him from running off alone."

Beatrice had been dismissive. "Seriously? He wouldn't do that. He's too crazy about Hannah to leave her."

"He said that he was going to take off with us or without us."

"And you believed him?"

"I did. He showed me his letter of resignation from the university. I knew he was going to submit it, no matter what I had to say about it."

The Bermans and the Silvers had lived together in the same apartment building in Elkins Park. They'd been neighbors separated by a landing at the top of a staircase, had spent dozens of cozy evenings agreeing about what was wrong with the world. Michael and Ted, both teachers, yearned for a life without classroom routines and suburban conformity.

"To tell you the truth, I thought it was just talk." Bea had said, pouring boiling water over tea bags. "I thought it was, you know, just the typical complaining that everybody does about his job. But it was *such* a good job."

Karen said, "He really didn't want it. He only stayed in grad school the last couple of months because he'd invested so much time writing the thesis that he wanted to finish it. The job in Abington was to teach the same course he'd been teaching as a graduate assistant, and he'd already had enough of that. Him quitting is nothing new; he'd been threatening to do it since we came to Elkins Park."

"But he took the job, didn't he."

"It was too good an offer to pass up," Karen had replied. "The weird thing is that he can actually teach, you know; he's a natural, he has the gift."

And they had liked his thesis and wanted him to continue for the Ph.D. They'd offered him the job in Abington to give him time to think things over. The job came with a good salary and was tenure-track. There was really no good reason for him *not* to take it, especially since he didn't have any other ideas.

That wasn't all of it, of course. Michael had also wanted out of their marriage - he'd wanted to cut all of his ties. She wouldn't discuss the matter with Beatrice, who would tell her husband Ted, Michael's bosom buddy. In fact, Karen has never discussed her marital problems with anyone, not even Michael. If you talk about things, they come true.

The first time he'd told her that he wanted a divorce had been before she became pregnant with Hannah. It had been winter, the second year of their marriage. They had been in their first year of graduate school, living in a one bedroom apartment near campus. "I'm not happy," he'd said. "I've been having these terrible doubts about us… for a long time. It isn't your fault."

Dry-eyed, seeing the bulk of the *Winnebago* in the rear-view mirror, she remembers that tears had spilled from her eyes.

"I know there's something wrong with me," he'd said. "I can't seem to be happy. Something isn't right, no matter what. It isn't fair to you, it's not right for both of us to be miserable when it's only me who can't be happy."

That's something she can't understand; how such a happy person could claim to be otherwise. He's so contradictory, so full of shit.

Immediately, she'd seen his *mea culpa* as a lie. Obviously, her husband found her wanting, otherwise he'd not be contemplating divorce. She knows that he wants more from her in bed. But that is just the way men are, or so she's been told. He'd waved that illustrated book at her, as a way of saying he wants her to be more sexy. Well, she is who she is. A lot of the positions that are drawn in the book are repulsive. They'd tried a few, but she'd found them embarrassing.

But what about Dean! What about yesterday! She hadn't even thought about what they were doing. It just happened, like a miracle.

Her tears had an effect. On the cold day when Michael first raised the subject, her woe had so disarmed him that he'd recoiled, allowing her to be alone until she regained her equilibrium, which took several days. Then, very carefully, a week or so later, on a frigid evening in the mountains of Central Pennsylvania, he'd said, "What I said the other day... I want to get divorced."

Her reaction had been more extreme the second time; she'd bawled. He'd dropped the matter for awhile. Crying had not been a ploy, really, she had not been *using* tears, she'd simply had no other way to respond to a man who said he loved her but wanted to leave her. Several weeks passed. Things between them had returned to a version of normal, and he'd said. "We should talk about this."

And that was when they had decided that the marriage needed a baby. Thank god. And now there's Hannah. And he has never raised the subject again.

Instead, he'd decided to leave her without getting a divorce.

It could just be just a phase. They say that every marriage goes through hard times. Time will heal this wound. That's what this whole adventure is about – time.

Bea had pressed the matter, "So how's it been going between you and Michael? You know..."

"Good," Karen had said. "Everything's fine."

"Can I give you a little advice?"

"Okay," Karen had said, stirring honey into her tea.

"It would be better if you didn't wait for him to decide. It's always better to be the one who makes the move. It's better to have your ducks in a row than to get pushed into limbo."

"Ducks?"

"Well, not ducks. You know what I mean. You don't want to be surprised. If it's going to end, let him get the surprise. You want to be the one in control."

"That sounds pretty cold."

Bea, sipping her unsweetened tea, had said, "Maybe so. But it's the way it is. A girl has to be smart."

Short Hose Dilemma

Michael likes driving. Road safety requires just enough concentration that the tumbling ideas in his mind recede to background noise, and the momentum under his control gives him a sense of purpose. True, the purpose is an easy one, merely a destination for tonight or tomorrow. But it is *his* purpose. Once there, he'll perhaps choose another destination - and that's what's so wonderful.

He wonders why Dean *has* to be in Culiacan. Some sort of appointment? What can that be about? Drugs? Dean seems so clean-cut, so all-American. Michael had been surprised when he had revealed himself as a pot smoker. But a lot of people under thirty years old are into it these days, especially the guys coming back from Vietnam. So maybe Dean is in the pot trade. He has money, that's for sure. He is vague about the owner of the *Winnebago*, claiming it's not his. But who knows?

Karen is keeping an eye on the wing mirror. Michael asks her, "What do you think of Dean?"

"I like him," she says.

"Me too," says Hannah from the backseat.

"How about you?" Karen asks. "What do you think of him?"

"He's seems like a good guy," says Michael. "He knows what he's doing. His equipment is all first class. But what a waste. I mean, all that equipment and all that gas for one guy and a dog? That bothers me."

"You're just jealous," she says.

"Are you kidding? What would I want with all that?"

"A shower. A big sink. A decent-sized refrigerator."

"Here's the thing about that," says Michael. "You get a bigger fridge and you buy more food. Pretty soon you're throwing food away. A small fridge is better."

"Still," she says. "It would be nice. A little luxury never hurt anyone."

"It depends on what you mean by luxury, doesn't it? I mean where do you draw the line?"

"At a shower ," she says.

"That's what campgrounds are for. Communal showers use much less water."

"And you could always go swimming," says Hannah.

"That's right, Hannah," says Michael. "Good thinking. How you doing back there?"

"Okay. Can I ride with Remus?" she asks. The dog had greeted Hannah as an old friend this morning.

"Maybe," says Karen. "I'll think about it."

"Please?"

"We don't know much about Dean," Michael says. "Maybe after we know him better."

"Or maybe Remus could ride with us. He could sit with me."

"We'll see," says Karen.

The dog's master seems seems like a steady guy. Michael respects the men who'd served in Vietnam, and he's embarrassed that he had not been among them, having consciously decided not to risk his life as a soldier in a stupid war. Like millions of other young American men, Michael had decided to avoid the draft. But it's a tender topic, especially these days. So, he will not ask Dean about his reasons for going into The Army and he does not expect Dean to ask him about why he had evaded the draft. They are two guys on the road in a foreign country, reason enough to give a compatriot the benefit of the doubt. Who knows? They might even become friends.

The war in Vietnam has affected everyone; as the war drags on, differences of opinion are becoming divisions between different kinds of Americans. Politics is no longer about being a Republican or a Democrat in a united country. Now that the afterglow of World War Two has faded, Americans are discovering new reasons to dislike each other.

Men returning from Vietnam face scornful World War Two veterans who look upon them as losers – long-haired freaks who take drugs, listen to bad music, and aren't manly enough to win a war. These are the Legionnaires who visit the local barbershop once a month to reaffirm their rectitude and reinforce their delusions, the generation of men who believe that America can do no wrong and deeply resent anyone who thinks otherwise. These are the men in charge.

News footage of Vietnam - body bags, napalm, helicopters in rice paddies – makes half the country angry. Anti-war images – marches, burning flags, flaming draft cards – incense the other half. A black man serves on the Supreme Court, outraging all the white people who think they are the only Americans with the right to wear the exalted robes. Impoverished black people live segregated from the mainstream in dense slums. All over the country, white people are in full flight from the brick cities and the black neighborhoods to the treeless subdivisions that were yesterday's farms. *Playboy Magazine* models display nipples and pubic hair. Women, liberated by The Pill, burn their brassieres, flaunting their sexuality and embarrassing their elders, people who can't say *'sex'* without blushing. Communes are sprouting in the Western States like hallucinogenic mushrooms on cow pats. America is fracturing.

Dean intrigues him because, unlike most Vietnam veterans, he is as cleancut as a toothpaste actor. The other veterans Michael knows try to be cool, to blend in with their long-haired contemporaries, to declare their difference from the men in charge by wearing beads, beards, and loose-fitting shirts.

As they travel the three hundred miles to Culiacan, the *Winnebago* is visible in the wing mirror most of the time. The cowboy proves himself a good driver, pulling close to the shoulder to let faster vehicles pass. Michael drives the same way, as conscious of the road behind as he is of the road ahead. It's an uneventful trip. The *Winnebago* is thirstier than his little *Dodge*, and they stop more often for gas than Michael ordinarily would. And the dog needs chances to pee. The final fifty miles twist through mountains, so they don't arrive at the commercial campground on the outskirts of Culiacan until quite late in the afternoon.

For the first time, he can't get the trailer close enough to the sewer inlet at his campsite to attach the five foot remnant of old hose that had been left in the bumper after the new, long one fell out on the way to Yosemite. Another reason they had left Catch-22 was because the holding tank under the trailer that captures water from the sink and toilet is almost full. So, as soon as he has a chance to inspect their assigned campsite, he lets Karen and Hannah out and drives the rig to the communal dumping station at the far end of the campground. When the tank is emptied, he shuts the flow valve, stows the remnant of hose inside the hollow bumper, and caps the end with fresh duct tape. He'd hoped to pass a place that sold camping supplies and replace the missing hose and bumper cap, but hasn't seen one yet. Tomorrow, he will explore Culiacan to find a supplier.

He returns to their space and unhitches the trailer, pleased by the hitch repair, by the way the chrome ball rises as the weight is removed. He levels the trailer and plugs in to the campground's electrical supply; their lights will burn brighter tonight.

Karen is taking a walk around the campground with Dean, watching Hannah and the dog as they explore. They are taking their time, stopping to chat with some of the other vagabonds, so he goes inside to relax with a Spanish language copy of *TIME* magazine that he'd bought at a gas station.

He looks at the pictures of familiar politicians and other famous people, learning a bit more Spanish as he reads the captions. The Watergate scandal dominates the magazine. Republican President Richard Nixon is hiring and firing lawyers on a weekly basis, doing a legal dance to avoid prosecution – impeachment by the House of Representatives – for paying clandestine operatives to steal from the Democratic Party's files in the *Watergate Hotel* during the 1972 campaign. Senate hearings revealed that Nixon used government agencies to conceal the crimes and to attack his enemies. Political heat, already stoked by the war, is fierce. The Spanish word for 'impeachment' is the same as it is in English.

Hannah and Karen return to the trailer. "I'll get supper started," says his wife. "We're having macaroni and cheese. Okay? And I'll open a can of green beans."

"Did you look at the showers? How are they?" he asks.

"The ladies' shower was clean."

"Good. Tomorrow we'll go looking for a hose in Culiacan. But it won't take all day. Hannah, maybe when we come back, you'll get a chance to play with the dog."

"He's not just a dog, Daddy. His name is Remus."

"You like him a lot, don't you?"

"Yes I do. He is so much fun. He likes to play with me."

"Well that's so nice," he says.

"There's no reason for all of us to go," Karen says. "We'll take our time here. I need to clean this place up; there's still sand from Catch-22 all over."

After they eat, as Karen helps Hannah prepare for bedtime, Michael takes a stroll around the crowded campground. The grounds are clean, with concrete hookup pads aligned in long rows across a few acres. All of the vehicles bear American license plates. There are a couple of converted VW vans, "hippie mobiles". A few spaces are occupied by hitch-hikers and bicyclists with bedrolls and tents. There are trailers, all bigger than his, camper-topped pickups like George's, and arvees, Dean's *Winnebago* the largest. He waves at a skinny guy perched inside the door of his van and says hello to a retired couple walking a pair of Dachshunds. Night has fallen, weak street lamps light the avenue.

Dean is sitting outside his *Winnebago* on a folding chair, a cigarette in one hand and a beer in the other. Remus, lying by his side, stands as Michael approaches.

"Some place," says Michael.

"It's more crowded than I would have thought," says Dean.

"I wouldn't want to stay here very long. Why is it you have to be here tomorrow night?"

"No real reason," he says. "But you don't have to hang out here to wait for me; you could just go on ahead tomorrow. We'll meet up in Oaxaca."

"No. That's all right," Michael says. "We have some shopping to do tomorrow. You know, groceries. And I have to find a replacement for my damned sewer hose. Karen wants to clean the trailer. So we'll be here tomorrow. If you're still going to leave the day after tomorrow, we'll still be able to travel together."

"Okay. Sounds like a plan."

"You know, " says Michael. "I was hoping you were meeting someone to buy some weed."

"Naah. Sorry," says Dean. "I could sell you a little of my stash."

"Well, thanks. I'll take you up on that. But I was hoping to score a little more, just to have it around. I've heard that the stuff grows wild in Mexico, that you can get it anyplace."

"I wouldn't want to deal with Mexicans. I hear the Mexican cops are cracking down on hippies."

"I think maybe I'll ask around here at the campground in the morning. Maybe somebody in one of the vans has enough to sell."

"You never know," says Dean.

Gender

Hannah is self-conscious about her hair. As a toddler, for a month or so, she'd walked around their apartment with a yellow baby blanket draped over her wispy hair, imitating women with thick, curling, blond tresses. Now her hair comes down over her ears like a girl's, and it's blond, but it still doesn't look like the pictures.

Mommy is washing her hair with baby shampoo. The shower makes a splashing sound on the cement floor and echoes off the walls. The morning sun comes in through the gap under the high roof and glows on the white and turquoise tiles. She watches how Mommy washes herself. Today, Mommy washes between her legs twice.

Mommy turns off the shower and they dry themselves with their towels. A lady comes in, hangs up her bathrobe, and turns on the shower. She is old, with short, mostly gray hair and a big, fat, saggy body. As Hannah and Mommy are putting on their clean clothes, the lady turns off the shower and starts to dry herself.

"And what's your name?" the lady asks her.

"Hannah Berman," she says.

"Well, hi Hannah."

"Hi," Mommy says. "Where are you from?"

"Michigan. You?"

"Pennsylvania. Where are you headed?"

"Mazatlan. And you?"

"Us too. We're going tomorrow."

Hannah enjoys the names of the Mexican towns, the sound of Spanish: Guaymas, Culiacan, Mazatlan. She says, "Mah-zot-LON."

The lady smiles. "I'm Gloria Baumgartner. Nice to meet you."

"I'm Karen Berman. Nice to meet you." Mommy smiles back, showing her nice teeth. Hannah still has little baby teeth.

"And how old are you," Gloria asks.

"Four," she says, and shows four fingers. She can count to a hundred and write the numbers.

"Well, good for you," she says. "I have granddaughters near your age." Then she asks Mommy, "You're here on vacation?"

"Yep," says Mommy.

"We're on a quest," says Hannah.

"Really," Gloria exclaims. "Well that's interesting. A quest for what?"

"It's not really a quest," says Mommy. "Just a long vacation. When it's over, my husband has to look for another job."

"I see. Well that's nice that you can do that at your age."

"I suppose it is," Mommy says.

Mommy is twenty-nine. Daddy is thirty. "How old are you?" Hannah asks.

"Ancient," says Gloria.

Gloria walks with them when they go outside the shower house. "This is me," Gloria says, and stops in front of a fifth wheeler, the kind of trailer that gets hitched inside the back part of a pickup truck. A green truck is parked nearby under a tree. "I've got to take Misty and Fergie for a walk," says Gloria.

"Are Misty and Fergie dogs?" Hannah asks.

"Yes they are. Wait here a minute and I'll bring them out."

They are wonderful little dogs, long and brown, called Dachshunds. They let her pet them. She can tell them apart because Fergie is skinnier and longer and has a male dog peepee, like Remus, who is also a male dog. Misty has a lot of nipples, enough to feed a lot of puppies.

"Can I come with you?" Hannah asks.

"Sure," says Gloria. "If it's all right with your Mommy."

"That's fine," Mommy says. "You'll bring her back soon. She hasn't had her breakfast."

"We won't be long," says Gloria.

Mommy goes to the trailer by herself, carrying their towels, and Hannah stays with Gloria and the dogs. They have to be careful walking in the street because the rigs are leaving to spend the day on the road. Tomorrow morning, they will get on the road to Mazatlan. They will go swimming there, Mommy says. Fergie and Misty pull at their leashes and Gloria has to keep untangling them. Fergie pees with his leg up, but Misty squats to do it.

"Why doesn't Misty pick up her leg?" she asks.

"Because she's a female. Males and females do things differently - even dogs."

Yes. When they grow up, girls are beautiful. But until then, they are like boys, except girls play with dolls and don't like to hurt other people. When boys grow up, they are big and strong and take charge of things.

"You remind me of my granddaughter," says Gloria.

"Is she four?"

"No. She's seven now. I miss her. Do you have a Grandma?"

"I have Nana and Grammy."

"I bet you miss them, don't you."

She's not sure, so she doesn't say anything.

"You know, I like little girls. Maybe you can keep me company."

"Okay," says Hannah. "Can I play with Fergie and Misty? Maybe Remus can come too."

"Who's Remus?"

"He's a Labrador Retriever. He lives in the *Winnebago*," she says, pointing to Dean's arvee.

"Oh. Well. That wouldn't be a good idea, in case they fight with each other. Misty and Fergie are small. A Lab could eat them up."

"No he wouldn't. Remus is nice. He never fights," she says. "And he only eats dog food. Sometimes lizards, but not dogs."

"Well, I think it's best if you play with Remus by himself. Okay?"

"Okay. Can I still play with Fergie and Misty?"

"Absolutely. I'll ask your Mommy."

When Gloria takes her back to their trailer, Gloria asks Mommy if it will be okay for her to come to their fifth-wheeler later on, she and her husband, whose name is Vic, will be glad for the company. Mommy says it would be just fine with her. Daddy is going to drive around looking for a hose and she's going to be busy, so that will be perfect.

After she has her *Cheerios*, Mommy combs and brushes her hair and fluffs it up with the blow dryer, which they can use now that they are plugged in at a campground. Mommy holds her up in front of the mirror in the bathroom so she can see how nice she looks.

"Wish me luck," Daddy says, and drives away in the car.

Mommy fills up a bag with her *Barbies* and coloring books and stuff and walks with her to the fifth-wheeler. She says to Gloria, "I'm going to wash the floor and clean all the cabinets. So - if you wouldn't mind - if Hannah could stay a couple of hours?"

Gloria says, "Take all day. We'll be just fine. Hannah can stay for lunch, if she likes."

"What do you say, kiddo?" Mommy asks her.

"Yes indeedy," she answers. That's how you say it when you think it's a really good idea.

Lust

Karen cleans the tiny trailer's interior in fifteen minutes. She changes out of her jeans and puts on her best, black panties. She puts her bra away with the rest of her underwear, leaving her tits free under the loose cotton sundress she decides to wear. In front of the mirror, she applies lipstick and eye liner, and gives her hair a final fluff with the blow dryer.

She takes a circuitous route to Dean's arvee, starting off in the opposite direction and coming back on the far street, with enough trees and vehicles between her and the Baumgartners' fifth wheeler to reduce the chances that she'll be seen. It's another bright, dry day in Western Mexico. At this campground, the vehicles park perpendicular to the streets, their hitches and hoods pointed out, ready for an easy getaway. Now that most people have departed, it's only a quarter full. She keeps an eye on the Baumgartner's trailer and sees no sign that she's been noticed.

The *Winnebago* has three doors, two in front and one on the side facing away from her own trailer and the Baumgartners'. She knocks.

She hears Remus woof twice before Dean opens the door. "Hi," he says.

"I thought I'd drop by and see how you're doing."

"Where are Michael and Hannah?"

"He went to Culiacan to buy a sewer hose. Hannah's spending the morning with a nice old couple and a pair of Dachshunds."

"So he'll be gone awhile?" Remus stands behind him, slowly wagging his tail.

"Uh huh," she says.

Dean is barefoot, wearing jeans and a black tee shirt. He looks down at her and she stares into his light blue eyes. For a moment, she thinks he's going to turn her away. Then he stands aside and says, "Remus. Outside. Guard."

The dog leaps out and sniffs her. She puts out her hand and the dog gives it a lick, as if to say, "I know you."

"Come on in," says Dean.

Inside, the *Winnebago* smells like pot. There are papers on the dining table. Dean goes immediately to them , gathers them up, places them inside a big manila envelope which he puts into a drawer.

"Have a seat," he says, gesturing at a bench sofa with nubby, green upholstery. "Can I get you something? Would you like some weed?"

"That would be nice," she says.

He takes a joint from from behind the narrow band of elastic that keep the joints from spilling out of his silver cigarette case. He lights up and they share it, getting near to the end when she says she's had enough. He stubs it out in an ashtray and looks at her, a slight smile on his face. His eyelashes are thick and bleached, soft frames around his eyes as he brings his face close to hers.

As they kiss, she feels a little dizzy from the smoke and the taste of his saliva. The muscles tighten all over her body and she feels a rush. "Can I see you? Can I look at you?" she asks.

"Naked?"

"Please," she says.

He strips and stands in front of her. His arms are tanned below the biceps. The hair around his penis is darker than the curls on his head. His cock is different from Michael's, curving upward in a slight arc. Michael's is straight as poker, a little shorter, maybe with a bigger glans. She can't be sure - for years, they have done it in the dark.

"Turn around," she says.

The smooth globes of his ass are beautiful, and she puts her palm at the small of his back and strokes the curve. "Now you," he says.

She stands, pulls the dress over her head, tosses it onto the sofa, and drops her already moist panties onto the floor. She looks down and sees that her nipples are flat and rubs her palms over them to wake them up, and they rise obediently.

He takes a stride toward her and bends over to kiss her nipples. She reaches for his cock and feels a rush across her shoulders and her stomach as she holds it. Inside, her belly clenches, a rush that makes her knees weak.

She leads him to the back of the arvee, to the bed, with sheets smoothed without a wrinkle, as if he's prepared it for inspection. She puts her knees on the mattress and spins to face him, puts her hands on his ribs and pulls him close, his cock hard and hot against her belly. She kisses him hungrily. He climbs onto the bed and lays on his back and she knows that he wants her to put it in her mouth. She puts her lips around the glans and sucks it, pours her spit onto it, covering the length of it with her mouth juice with her fingers. She knows how hard to tease it, sensing the needs of his cock as if she's always known, finds the spot that makes him writhe and groan.

Then he puts a hand on her shoulder and pushes her away and she falls onto her back. She spreads her legs and is glad that he doesn't fool around, but drops onto his hands and probes her with his blind cock, searching for the way in. She puts her hand between her legs and aims him him onto her juicy pussy, and he enters her right away, fast, smooth, then deeper, pushing. She needs to squeeze him, to feel him, and she clasps his sides between her thighs and plants her heels on his ass and urges him deeper so that she can feel his weight on her clit. And she comes! Oh god! So fast. So soon.

More. She needs more, and she lets him fuck her, lets him pound her as hard as he can. She grunts like an animal with each powerful thrust. Then he goes faster until he can take it no more and she FINALLY feels his cock, the whole of it, filling her, swelling, throbbing. And she comes again, deeply, slowly.

Carefully, he settles on his forearms and lays his head next to hers on the pillow.

She's not quite done with him. She comes again, squeezing his cock so hard that she pushes it out.

"Oh my," she chortles. It's so funny. She feels so good.

Yin, Yang and Valentines

Culiacan reminds him of Tijuana – a warren of crowded streets and pastel storefronts. Stupidly, in his hurry to get away, he'd left the hose inside the bumper. Now he has to explain what he wants. He draws a picture for the man behind the counter at an automotive parts store. The guy shakes his head. "*No lo tenemos,*" he says. They don't have it, nor does he think it can be found in Culiacan. He has no suggestions. Referring to his dictionary, Michael asks about plumbing supplies and gets the guy to look up an address and write it down. Then some real customers come in and Michael has to leave before he can get directions. So he returns to the car and drives around for half an hour until he finds the address of the plumbing supply store. Same story, "*No lo tenemos.*" Any ideas? None whatsoever.

He makes sure his car is locked and takes a walk onto the town square, a well worn park with benches lining walkways that meet at a bandstand in the center. It's midday, and the dense shade under the trees has attracted a lot of people, some with their lunches. He sits at a vacant bench, reluctant to return to the campground.

His nature is masculine, to cause change, to make things happen, *yang*. Karen's nature is feminine, adaptive, *yin*. In Taoism, opposites are inseparable. In the moment, the rock and the water flowing around it are a balanced whole. A man should understand that his troubles arise from doing too much – rushing too hard. A woman's troubles arise from accepting too much, lest she get swept away or broken apart. Misery is the consequence of internal imbalance - yielding too much or causing too much. Each partner must find internal balance before he or she can be satisfied within the relationship. A woman and a man will both be miserable if one does not resist enough or the other pushes too hard.

Perfection is represented by the yin-yang design, , the black and white disk bisected by the sinuous curve, the boundary that represents the *Tao*. At the center of any entity, a man or a woman for example, the opposite nature abides, shown as a disk of the opposite color in the center of each curved teardrop. A bad marriage has too much black or too much white, one side squeezing the other. For the one being squeezed, the area of the marriage disk is too small, causing the person's central disk of the opposite color, which cannot be altered, to seem disproportionally large. The squeezer occupies too much space, with a disproportionally small disk of the opposite color inside his or her teardrop.

Michael thinks that Karen yields too much space, and that he is pulled into it by her vacuity. He needs someone to push back, to make things happen. Michael feels as if he has been sucked in, his skin stretched like a balloon's.

She's more like a cloud than a rock. No matter what he says or does, she accepts it. He espouses, she agrees. He goes, she goes along.

A boy, with a tray positioned across his chest, comes along the walkway and stands in front of Michael. A few boxes of *Chiclets* chewing gum are arranged on the tray. He says, "*Chicle. Tengo chicle. Diez centavos.*"

"No, gracias," says Michael. He buys only what he seeks. He is leery of transactions that he does not initiate, no matter how trivial, even for a box of *Chiclets*. He is repelled by advertising in any form. The more forceful the sales pitch, the less likely he is to buy. The relationship between a seller and a buyer is a form of the Tao, a transaction.

"*Solo diez centavos*," says the boy.

Ten Mexican cents are worth less than half an American nickel. The boy is virtually giving the gum away. He is a skinny waif with dust in his black hair. Clearly, he needs every coin that comes his way. By Mexican standards, Michael is filthy rich. He and the boy are way out of balance. But he overcomes his instinctive sales resistance and hands the boy a peso coin, ten times the asking price, minutely shifting the Tao between them toward a better balance.

Awareness of the other person is the key to finding the good balance. With the *Chiclet* vender, it's simple; he's poor and needs a peso.

Michael does not make Karen happy. When he asks about her feelings, she shrugs and says she doesn't know. Karen is never particularly happy or sad. She doesn't express any desires. The only times she has ever been clear about her feelings were the times, years before, when he had broached the subject of divorce. She had reacted as if he'd kicked her in the stomach. Clearly, he knows how to make her miserable. Michael is incapable of inflicting pain; he certainly can't kick his wife.

But she won't, or can't, tell him what he ought to do to please her. She won't talk about their marriage, about how she feels. He doesn't know whether she is vague because she doesn't know how she feels, or because she is one of those passionless people with only vague feelings, or because her feelings paralyze her, or if she's using her blandness to wound him. So he can't *do* anything. Because his nature is to make things right by doing, he is frustrated. This is his quandary - he cannot make their relationship any better, but divorce would probably make things worse, especially for Hannah.

Too, he has a guilty conscience. Like a romantic lead in a movie, he'd gushed devotions in the early months of their relationship. He'd been persuasive, the initiator, compelled by lust. She'd agreed to be in love, and had opened her legs for him, the one special man who would be her husband, the father of her children, her partner unto death. He had sworn that he was that man. If he no longer loves her, then he is breaking the promise, and a good man keeps his promises.

He tries not to be phony, tries to be unpretentious, tries to speak truthfully. People who are changeable are inherently phony. If he is no longer in love with his wife, that means he'd lied just to have sex with her. He's a phony. But, he does not *feel* in love. The opposite, in fact - he resents her. Sometimes, he wishes she'd vanish. He doesn't say he loves her anymore, but shows devotion with sex, by staying married, by caring for Hannah. But is devotion love? Does the difference matter?

Love, too, has an image of perfect design, a Valentine's Day heart. A thousand movies and love songs say that true love endures, that the two halves form a permanent unity. He and Karen, having seen all the movies, are convinced that married people naturally stay together, that separating the halves violates the natural order.

But, by far, the most painful guilt would result from causing Hannah and Karen to suffer. In this case, if he were to "just do it," he'd be committing a sin - not a religious sin, but a human one. His conscience argues for him to stay in the marriage, with the promise of punishing guilt were he to break it apart.

There, on a bench, are two teenagers in love. They are not touching, but are completely attentive to each other. It probably won't last. All around the park, men and women are in separate clusters; the men in self-important twos, threes and fours; the women in little covens watching boisterous children. The teenagers will soon be lovers, and that will change them. Then they will be parents, and that will change them. If he returns to the park in a few years, the boy will be hanging out with his pals, she with the mothers, each a different person from the love struck teenager on a park bench.

He is fascinated by couples, watches them, curious about the interplay of *yang* and *yin* between two people. Just as intriguing are the mysteries inside himself, where the equilibrium morphs, as life goes on, as circumstances change, moment by moment.

The moments, the instants, obsess him because they won't return, and there is so much to know about each one, so many knots to unravel, so much beauty. He loves every tree, every rock, every cloud. Like normal people, he used to live unaware of the passage of time, going from task to task, focused on the doing. Of late, when he is alone, the instant death of each moment makes him want to stop time.

Road Mothers

Karen washes up in Dean's bathroom, using his only towel.

It would be nice to live in the *Winnebago*. She could be with a man who laughs at her jokes and makes love to her as if he loves her, a good-looking man she'd be proud to stand beside. Hannah would have Remus. Not that it could happen. It's just a fantasy. But wouldn't it be nice? Doesn't she have a right to a little happiness?

There's a window in the bathroom, and she peers through it, seeing no one afoot around the Baumgartners' fifth-wheeler or their own trailer.

When she leaves the bathroom, Dean is seated at the table, back in his jeans and tee shirt, smoking a cigarette, a pack of *Marlboros* and a tin ashtray in front of him. He says, "Would you like something? Something to drink? I can make coffee."

She puts on her clothes as he watches. "That sounds nice, but I better go. I have to check on Hannah," she says, taking a cigarette from his pack and lighting up.

"Will you come back?"

"Soon," she says. "Keep the coffee hot."

She has become comfortable in campgrounds, understands how they work, where to look for the quirks, how people are supposed to behave. Everyone is a stranger, no

149

one knows anyone. Midday is the quiet time at a campground, after folks have taken to the road, before another bunch arrive to spend the night. Right now, in Culiacan, only a half-dozen sites are occupied, so she has the street to herself as she walks to the Baumgartners' site. It feels slightly naughty to be smoking a cigarette while she walks outside. At college, it had been against the rules for women to smoke in public.

She feels all twinkly. My God!

Parked fifth-wheelers appear a little precarious to her, off balance, with their heavy snouts supported by stilts. The dachshunds are tied to long leashes attached to the back bumper. Unlike the Bermans' trailer, which is is all white, with a little bit of gold vinyl trim on the door and windows, the Baumgartners' trailer is almost twice as long as the Bermans' box, pale tan, with yellow and brown trim. Gloria Baumgartner invites her inside when she knocks on the door.

Hannah is at the formica table with a coloring book.

Gloria introduces her husband, Vic, a big, white-haired man wearing polyester pants and a golf shirt. He's sitting in a chair with a magazine in his lap.

"Scuse me for not getting up," he says.

"Vic's been having some leg problems," Gloria says.

"Hi. I'm Vic," he says

She goes to him and shakes his hand. "Hi, I'm Karen Berman. Thanks for putting up with Hannah."

"Please. It's our pleasure. We like having kids around," he says. "Don't we Gloria?"

"Nice ones," says Gloria. "We like nice little girls like Hannah."

"Hey, kiddo," Karen says. "How you doin'?"

"I had chocolate milk," says Hannah. "Gloria made it."

"I hope you don't mind," says Gloria.

"Not at all." But it hadn't occurred to Karen to mention their food precautions. What if Gloria had fed her something that wasn't sterilized? "We are really careful about the food down here, though. Did she have anything else?"

"Two cookies. I had two *Oreos*," Hannah confesses.

Karen is relieved. "They're okay," she says.

"You're right to be careful. Us too," says Vic. "You can pick up some really nasty bugs down here. Last year, we had to take some idiot hitchhiker we met to the hospital. One of those hippies. Right, Gloria?"

Gloria nods in agreement. "I wonder what happened to him. Jesus, he was so sick. I wouldn't be surprised if he died."

Vic says, "You can die, that's for sure. Especially if you get the amoebas. They got no cure for that one, amoebic dysentery. It'll kill ya."

Gloria says, "Hannah says you're heading to Oaxaca?"

"Uh huh. Have you been there?"

"We've been there a lot," says Gloria. "You should stay at *La Resolana*."

"Is that a campground?"

Gloria and Vic Baumgartner come from Flint, Michigan. He used to work for an automobile manufacturer. She had been at home, raising three daughters, during the years after Vic got out of the the service, the postwar years, when TV was new. They spend half of each year living in their trailer, touring the National Parks, visiting relatives. As it turns out, they spend the winter months in Oaxaca every year.

Gloria describes *La Resolana*, "It's in a garden, surrounded by a wall, part of an estate. They have gardeners working all day long, really taking care of the plants, sweeping up. There are only a dozen sites, and they're almost all under trees. Vines grow up the walls, poinsettia and bougainvillea. The colors! You should definitely try to get a site there. We'll be there. We have a space reserved."

"How does that sound to you, Hannah?" says Karen.

"Nice," says Hannah.

"Here," says Gloria, "Let me get you their phone number. Call them and see if you can get a space. Trust me, you'll be glad." She consults her personal directory, copies the number onto a sheet of letter paper, and hands it to Karen.

"Terrific," says Karen. She'll have Michael call the campground. And she'll have to tell Dean.

"Come on, kiddo," Karen says. "Let's go see if Remus is home."

She thanks the Baumgartners once again as they are on their way out.

"Anytime," Gloria says.

No More Puppies For Misty

Misty had growled at her, that's why Gloria tied her up with Fergie. Hannah best stay away from her, Gloria says. "She hasn't gotten over her puppies yet," says Gloria said. "And she's fixed now... no more puppies for Misty."

"How did you fix her?" Hannah asks.

"We gave her an operation. Took out some of her girl parts."

"Did it hurt?"

"Naah. She got over it easy. But she hasn't been the same since we sold her puppies."

"Is Fergie her husband?"

"You could say that. They're more like friends."

That's how it is. When you grow up, you have a best friend and get married.

As she walks with Mommy to the *Winnebago*, she scans the ground for a stick she can throw for Remus. When they knock on Dean's door, Remus is so happy to see her that it makes her feel happy too.

Mommy says, "If you stay out of the street, you can play outside with Remus. I'm going to be right here watching out the windows, right here if you need me. I'm going to have a cup of coffee. Okay, kiddo?"

Cowardice

Having failed in his quest for a sewer hose, after his time alone in the park, Michael returns to the car.

The thing of it is, he feels so much more at ease when he doesn't have to contend with people. And that's another source of guilt, the fact that he's happiest by himself. He likes being with Hannah, but a child demands so much attention. And you have to be especially careful of what you say and how you say it. It's wearing.

As for Karen, her constantly detached presence is like an old wound that never quite heals. When she's angry, she doesn't say so. And she never says that she loves him anymore. She doesn't say anything interesting. She adds nothing to his life. She bores him. He has never said so to her, it is a hurtful thing to say, but he has admitted it to himself - she does not interest him. He'd be pleased never to have to spend another hour of his life with her. Maybe she'll be struck by lightning or fall out of a boat.

These silent betrayals are just more straws on top of the guilt pile. What sort of person is he?

As he had done in Guaymas, he takes the opportunity to drive around Culiacan on his own, along streets of one-story buildings and occasional palm trees where walls topped with broken glass shield the private houses. The shops and businesses are clustered on tired avenues, and

157

there's a church every few blocks. Then he finds himself on a dirt street that looks like a town in a cowboy movie, with swinging saloon doors and covered boardwalks. Until this moment, he'd believed such towns only existed in the movies. He will walk on the boardwalks and see what's going on. He parks at the corner.

Women, whores he supposes, are lounging in front of a couple of the saloons that line both sides of the street. So this is Culiacan's Red Zone, its *Zona Rosa*. In the USA, people are more ashamed of their baser urges, puritanical, enforcing secrecy on purveyors and customers alike. In Mexico, apparently, sinners absolve themselves in confessionals and return to the public red zones when necessary. This might be a place where he can buy some weed.

He walks along both sides of the street, looking over the tops of the doors as he passes each establishment. At this time of day, they are mostly empty. Jukeboxes play brassy *mariachi*, rock and roll, or soulful ballads. He steps into the place that looks busiest, where he'll be less conspicuous.

Cerveza is the only thing he knows how to order, so he steps to the bar, puts down a twenty *peso* note, and asks for a beer. The bartender puts a cold bottle and a tall glass in front of him.

A man wearing a black shirt comes to stand beside him. "Hallo, Mister," he says. He's about Michael's age, a head shorter, with a couple of day's black stubble on his cheeks and chin. There is a dance floor between the bar and a staircase on the other side of the large room. A few men wearing straw sombreros, farm workers who remind him of Fernando, are clutching bored looking women, shuffling around the floor. He guesses they have paid to dance with the women, unable to afford the money to take them upstairs. One of the men is barely moving his feet, grinding his pelvis into a woman wearing a floral print dress. Two men standing at the foot of the stairs, bouncers or pimps, are looking his way, watching him and the man in black. He feels outnumbered.

"*Ola,*" says Michael.

"What you want?" the fellow demands.

"*Nada,*" he says. So much for being inconspicuous.

"*Que deseas?* What you want?" He has a brazen manner, a menacing swagger, as if he'd enjoy slicing you open with a switchblade. The guy makes eye contact with the fellows at the foot of the stairs, then turns his attention back to Michael.

 "Nothing. Just a beer," Michael says.

"*Drogos? Quieres drogos? Mujeres?*"

Michael is embarrassed that his desires are so obvious. Does he want drugs? Yes? Does he want women? Yes. But not from this guy. He has the sense that the man and his friends would sooner rob him than sell him something. He's made a bad mistake.

"*No, gracias,*" he says.

The man finds this annoying, as if he knows that Michael is bullshitting and does not like it. The guy moves closer, and says, "Mister. What you want? I get you everything. Women? Drugs? Everything. What you want?"

The music changes from a ballad singer to a *mariachi* band. The other two have decided to join the conversation, looking at him and the man in black as they walk toward the bar between the pathetic couples on the dance floor. Clearly, he's about to be surrounded by a crew of thugs on their turf. Time to leave.

"*Adios,*" he says. Leaving the bottle of beer and his change, he walks away with long strides, out through the swinging doors, to the sunlit main street of Culiacan's *Zona Rosa*.

He hurries to the corner where he left the *Dodge*. As he gets near the car, he hears someone yell, "*Eres un hijo de puta.*" He looks over his shoulder and sees that the three are now on the boardwalk, watching him, seemingly ready to give chase. One of them had just called him a bad name - *puta* means *whore*. Big deal. He unlocks the car, gets behind the wheel, pulls the door closed and locks it immediately as he turns the key in the ignition. He pulls away from the parking space and has to drive past them. As he does, through the closed window, he hears another shout, another insult, but he cannot make out the words.

He finds the main highway without very many false turns and heads back to the campground on the outskirts of the city.

He is a coward, he knows. It's not just that he runs away from physical fights, he even lacks the courage to tell his wife the truth about his feelings for her.

Night Visitors

A round midnight, in their bed, Hannah in the bunk above, Michael can't sleep. Karen sleeps with her left side along the front wall of the trailer. His right side is toward the middle of the cube, so he does not have to climb over her when he leaves the bed. His clothes are in an overhead compartment at the back. Trying not to make noise, he puts on his jeans and a sweatshirt, slips into his sandals, and leaves them to take a walk around the campground and have a cigarette.

This campground is laid out as a quarter-mile long oval, with hookup sites along both sides, and a long avenue lined with sites down the middle, room for a couple of dozen different kinds of travelers. There are only a few vacant spaces. His site and Dean Scanlon's *Winnebago* are parked five sites apart on the same side of the oval. Light seeps into the night around the *Winnebago's* curtained windows. There's a big, dark, late model car parked in front of it. He looks at the license plate, reading it in the vague light of a distant street lamp - Mexico City.

There's a lot fishy about Dean Scanlon. Yet, he's a nice guy, and it's better to travel with someone in case you run into trouble or need a hand. And Hannah is in love with the guy's dog. He's interesting, easy to talk to, and he's got some good pot.

So who drove from Mexico City to rendezvous with Dean? The presence of the car suggests that the cowboy's trip has a purpose that, it now seems, is connected to people who conduct their business in the dark of night. What is Dean? A criminal? An undercover cop? Maybe he's still in the Army. Except for his curly locks, he seems very soldierlike. And that *Winnebago*! A government that could afford *B-52s* and helicopters wouldn't mind the cost of a giant arvee. If he is in the Army, why is he lying about it?

At a site on the other side of the oval, a fellow sits in front of a one-man tent. He's in the lotus position, cross-legged, bare-foot, hands in his lap. He doesn't move as Michael approaches and passes by. His eyes are closed.

Michael often meditates. He repeats his mantra silently, the word "one," with each exhalation. He used to do it in his office on the campus when he was not counseling students or marking papers. In those circumstances, the practice had helped him get through the tedious afternoons. And he's gotten into the habit of repeating his mantra during his sleepless nights. Sometimes it works for him, but not usually. Most of the time, he can't stop the rush of thoughts that bounce through his mind, but the meditation can sometimes slow down the ricochets.

He returns to the trailer and reenters as quietly as he left it. He returns his clothes to the overhead and climbs back into bed. Karen hasn't moved. She always sleeps soundly.

One….. One….. One….. One…..

Tomorrow, they will drive to Mazatlan, then Guadala-jara. The roadmap of Mexico he keeps in the glove compartment. Then on to Mexico City, then Oaxaca.

One….. One…..

Wasn't there a battle fought near here? Matamoros? He'd read about it in his ROTC military history class. As an undergraduate male at a Land Grant college, he'd been required to take six credits of ROTC. They'd made him a student officer, but demoted him after he'd marched his platoon to the edge of the duck pond.

One….

One way or another, even though he hadn't actually been in the US Army, it has been a constant influence, compelling him to make choices *to-avoid* rather than choices *to-achieve*. He's been playing defense all of his life.

One….

He had been on the verge of flunking out as a college freshman. He went to the Armed Forces recruitment center and returned with the sign-up papers. But his mother had dissuaded him, weeping bitter tears at the prospect of him quitting school. If he'd joined-up when he'd wanted to, he might have been out before the war in Vietnam got out of hand. Maybe he would have been in battles. What was that like? Would he have been brave?

One…..

Dean had been in Vietnam. He is brave.

One…..

Michael is a coward. Coward. Coward!

One…

Karen had not wanted sex tonight.

One… One… One…

Patience Monroe, naked, smiling.

Like Adornments On A Snowflake

Mazatlan reminds him of Miami Beach with more colorful wares for sale in the tourist shops. The campground where they've parked the trailer and *Winnebago* share the beach with two hotels. Vendors tread through sand selling *serapes* and pinwheels. Michael is sitting in one of the three beach chairs they've carried from their trailer. He has brought *The I Ching* onto the beach and is thumbing through it. Karen is standing in the mild surf, teaching Hannah to swim. Hannah is enjoying herself. All is well. Dean and Remus are in the arvee.

Change is constant, whether you make it or wait to meet it. Much of the *I Ching's* text is baffling, metaphorical, with references to ancient farming or warfare. He's just a traveling schoolteacher from Philadelphia and can't make sense of important passages. He still cannot frame the question, still doesn't know what he wants to know. The more a person *does,* the more changes he both confronts and creates, like the way water's velocity affects the ripples around a rock . Therefore, if he is to err, then it is best to make the fewest waves, to err on the side of doing little.

The West Pointers and business executives who got us into Vietnam ought to have read some Taoist thinking before they declared war against people who lived halfway around the world. Lyndon Johnson would have been wiser to have consulted Lao Tsu than Robert McNamara. The men in Hanoi are inclined by their philosophy to put great store in setting traps and snares, whilst the generals in Washington, with enormous destructive power at their command, look for ways to use it. They have gotten us into an awful situation and cannot admit it. Evil at home and abroad are the results of the American government's view of its role in the world. Now, almost a decade since Johnson's initial stupidity, the Nixon government is chewing off its limbs.

That's a difference between Taoists and people who believe in a mysterious evil force – the devil. In Taoism there are no gods or devils, just us folks. People who make bad decisions create unnatural circumstances: misery, suffering and ugliness. All of us - whether a General, a Wife, or a Husband - have the potential for evil, all of us make choices, all of us can inflict misery. Evil is a result, not a cause.

Michael is force without direction. He needs *to do*. But what to do? What to be? Shoo be do, shoo be dee. He's on a road to somewhere, on asphalt and dirt, doing by moving, going to places that are just places, mere arrival being the extent of his ambitions. But it's still him who's here, wherever he goes.

What should be his ambition? What are his talents? He does not think that bullshitting is a means of survival worthy of his potential. There are professions available to him that require the gift of articulation by itself, like salesmen, lawyers, actors, politicians, and advertising agents. None of that is for him; he does not want to use himself for dubious reasons. He won't work for bad purposes as people in the talking professions are often compelled to do. Not him, not if he can help it.

What's left for him, then, but to be a writer? He's written a few feeble short stories, but they have little merit and he knows it. He has no idea whatsoever of what to write about or of how to go about it, nor does he have an idea how to get paid as a writer.

The passages in the *I Ching* that he understands best are reminders to observe nature and take its meaning: to observe water and rock and know the benefits of peacefulness, to marvel at trees and the flight of birds, to hear the waves and buzzing insects. We should not be brutal to the living world. This is the part he gets.

Ugliness is a form of evil. If one is to cause change, then the desired result should be beautiful. This is an artist's motive. *The I Ching*, in every hexagram, suggests that the best path creates the good and the beautiful while doing the least harm. But how? He does not know his capabilities, what to do with his life. It's as if he is going to get just one chance to know the future. If tossing the coins is ever going to work, an extremely unlikely possibility, then it should work the first time. And if he frames the question properly, once should be enough.

He doesn't want to admit it, but as things stand, he'll probably go back to teaching, a less exalted form of talking, but still bullshit. He does not value what he knows, nor his talent for captivation; he can hold a class's attention, but for what purpose? Knowledge is personal, warped by other knowledge and woven with the threads of a person's life. He doesn't know how to share what he knows, doesn't feel that he himself understands the little he's learned in a lifetime. He would be arrogant were he to talk about it. Regardless, in the end, he'll probably be collecting a teacher's salary somewhere. But that's what he's just given up! That's exactly the work he'd run from!

For people like Patience Monroe, the questions don't seem troubling. For Michael, the conundrums proliferate like adornments on a snowflake. But they don't seem to get in Patience's way. For her, for now, she can be of the moments. She walks along a quay and finds an afternoon lover. And then walks away to do her shopping for a cruise to Panama, free, without entangling relationships. Good for her. Shoo be do, shoo be dee.

Karen and Hannah return from the pool of chlorinated water. Michael enjoys toweling his daughter's head, appreciates the trust she has in him, her acceptance, her sense of safety under his hands.

Karen asks, "Hannah, do you want to build a sand castle?" They have brought a blue plastic pail and a tin shovel with them.

"I do," says Hannah. She squats and shovels small loads of sand into the pail.

Lao Tzu said, the value of a vessel is in its emptiness.

"You can mold it better in the wet sand," Michael says. "You should get closer to the water. We'll watch you from here."

Hannah likes the idea and toddles off. How marvelous, that her beautiful little legs work, how eagerly she plays. It's a miracle. Five years ago she hadn't existed – now there's a person called Hannah Berman. Amazing.

"Do you want to stay?" Karen asks. "I think I've had enough. I'm going back."

"What about lunch?" he asks.

"Why don't I make some sandwiches and bring them back?" she says.

"That would be fine. Thanks."

"I'll be awhile, though. I have to take care of a few things."

"Like what?"

"Just personal stuff. I could use some time alone."

"Okay," he says. "Take your time."

Tribes

In Guadalajara, city traffic is as heavy as Philadelphia's, with numerous road signs pointing to places with exotic names. There are tall buildings in *El Centro*. On the ring road, as planned, Michael allows the *Winnebago* to overtake him so that Dean can lead them to the campground specified on his itinerary.

It bothers Michael that he has yet to find a sewer hose. He's had no luck in the auto supply stores of Guaymas, Culiacan, Mazatlan, and Tepic. If he can't find a place that sells accordion hose in Guadalajara, his last hope is Mexico City.

The Guadalajara campground is a well-ordered place with a powerful *Norte Americano* vibe: big trailers and arvees, many with tended garden patches out front and short flag poles flying the Stars and Stripe, a trailer park with an army base tidiness. The majority of the trailers are the expensive *Airstreams*, made of polished aluminum like fuselages, aerodynamically rounded at both ends. These flashy, highly-functional trailers are the brand preferred by ex-Army officers. Surely, these well equipped denizens of the Gringo Trail must have a way to satisfy their resupply requirements.

On their walk to the pool, Michael observes the placement of sewer hookups and considers stealing a hose. If he can't buy one tomorrow, how terrible would it be to take one from somebody else? Michael has never stolen anything, but surely such a theft would be relatively inconsequential. Most of these people, he rationalizes, probably have spares for everything.

He sits in a lounge chair on the pool apron, near a shuffleboard court, and opens *The Teachings of Don Juan*, in which Carlos Castaneda reports out-of-body experiences while eating peyote mushrooms under the tutelage of a Yaqui Indian shaman. Michael is intrigued by the witch doctor's reverence for nature, by the idea that people can purify their souls, take drugs, and inhabit the bodies of wild animals. He doubts that the author actually became a raven, but the notion appeals to him. Imagine - to fly like a bird while in a total trance, safe in his corporeal self, as his mind guides the movements of a raven on the wing.

He watches his wife and daughter playing in the pool, enthralled by Hannah's happy dog paddle.

One of the men on the shuffleboard court approaches him. "Care to grab a pole?" he says.

"Sorry? A pole?" says Michael.

"Yeah. Can you play shuffleboard? Nestor had to leave all of a sudden."

"I've played some on a table, but I've never played this game."

"So you know the rules?"

KNOTS

"I guess."

"Come on then. We need a fourth."

The three men are in their late-forties, having served their twenty years in the military, now living on American government pensions South Of The Border, where the *pesos* are cheap. They introduce themselves, offer him a beer, and hand him a pole. He manages to score a few points, but loses most rounds.

Michael's straight brown hair covers his ears. He wears a blue work shirt rolled to his elbows, blue jeans, sandals. Their hair is short and bristly, and their clothes are made of polyester. We belong to different tribes, with our own totems and badges.

His opponent, the man he stands beside when it is their turn to push the quoits, is a fellow named Jerry. As Michael now expects at any campground, Jerry asks where he is from, where he is going, what he does for a living, typical campground talk.

"I used to be teacher," he says. "I'm not sure what I'm going to do next."

There is uneasiness between Americans like Michael, who are ashamed of their government's bellicose foreign policy, and those like these retired servicemen who react to the anti-war factions with outraged pride. These are patriarchal men who respect authority and tend to react to disagreements as if they are disobedience.

"So? What kind of teacher?"

"Speech, mostly. I taught how to give speeches."

"That's interesting," says Jerry.

"Yes it is. I suppose. I managed to save up some money and decided to give myself a break, maybe look around for something different. I got tired of the teaching."

"Hmm," says Jerry.

American anger has been swelling in a crescendo without any prospect of a climax. War news - body bags, napalm, helicopters in rice paddies – makes half the country angry. Anti-war news – flaming flags, flaming draft cards, marches – incenses the other half. The culture gap is widening, the tribes reflected in politics, with the pro-war people tending Republican and anti-war people Democratic, even as the Watergate hearings are polarizing the tribes even farther.

Michael respects military men, does not blame them for the war, thinks of them as instruments of policy, not as the deciders. Whatever they may have done in the service of their country, it had not been their idea to make war. As the war in Vietnam intensified during the 1960s, his admiration for American servicemen had increasingly been infused with sympathy.

One of the differences between Michael's tribe and the one to which these ex-servicemen belong is the idea of obedience, a gap between Americans that has been widening since the mid-Sixties. Americans who are raised inside hierarchies of authority find military service congenial, accepting the notion that someone else has the right to tell them what to do, proud to do their duty. For Michael, whose parents had expected him to make good choices, unquestioned obedience is not a virtue but an abdication of the obligation to choose between right and wrong. These days, a swelling minority of Americans, longhairs like Michael, resist obedience to the Federal Government's efforts to order the world, appalled by the consequences - bloodshed and misery.

His motives for taking teaching jobs with draft exemptions had, to a degree, included this resistance to authority and to his belief that men in high positions are as likely to make mistakes as anyone else. Sometimes the mistakes are terrible, sowing evil.

But it was more complicated than that. Certainly, he had avoided putting himself in the way of flying bullets – and that is nothing more or less than cowardice. It troubles him that he has not proven himself as a brave, red-blooded American man. Which had been the stronger incentive for him – cowardice or loathing for the war? When he was still draft bait, he'd believed that wearing a uniform would implicate him in the murder of strangers on behalf of rich people even more cowardly than he. But isn't that self-serving rationalization? What of his duty to his country? He had chosen to be safe while his brothers had been in mortal combat.

He knows that the American soldiers still in harm's way in Southeast Asia are at the tip of a multi-million man enterprise of supply and communications, that men in danger from an enemy are a small minority of those who wear the uniform. This fellow Jerry seems too old and soft to have been holding a rifle in Khe San, but there is no doubt that he knows how to handle a shuffleboard pole

Karen and Hannah leave the pool.

Jerry expertly knocks Michael's quoit out of scoring position.

"Nice shot," says Michael. "Gotta go now. Thanks for the game."

"Okay. Thanks for playing."

"Can I ask you something? Do you know anyone who has some accordion hose to spare? For my sewer hookup. I'd like to buy about ten feet of it."

"I'll ask around," says Jerry. "Will you be here tomorrow?"

"I will. I plan to spend the day looking for some hose, driving around Guadalajara until I find some. But my wife will be here. Karen, this is Jerry – a hell of a shuffleboard player."

Dean walks by with Remus on a long leather leash. Hannah, clutching a towel over her tiny shoulders, scampers to greet her friend. The girl and the dog greet each other joyfully, as if they have been separated for a month.

"Come on, kiddo," says Karen. "Let's get you dressed."

"Remus! To me," says Dean. The dog instantly turns away from Hannah to stand in front of his master, obediently awaiting his next command.

///

He can make do without a longer hose, having one is not essential, but the fact that he is still missing a piece of his portable house is a nagging annoyance, an awareness of incompleteness. Too, the quest for better plumbing gives him an excuse to be by himself.

The auto and plumbing supply stores in Guadalajara are more widely disbursed than they had been in the smaller cities where he'd tried to buy a replacement hose. It takes Michael most of the day, consulting the phone book and a local street map, fighting traffic in the crowded streets, to discover that four-inch diameter accordion hoses are not on offer.

Late in the afternoon, after he returns, while Karen and Hannah are at the pool, he is stretched out on the sofa bench inside their trailer, reading a translation of the *Tao Te Ching* by Lao Tzu. The ancient sage advised humility, patience, and reverence for the unknowable, invisible, undetectable, irresistible Tao. Tao is a concept: nowhere and everywhere, order and chaos, a theory of active, con-

179

tinuing creation and destruction - change. The effort to understand it is the path, the way - at once the goal and the struggle. Understanding the Tao is impossible, but the achievement of a peaceful spirit is only possible if a person tries, so wrote Lao Tzu.

He is interrupted by someone knocking on the trailer door. It is Jerry of the shuffleboard, with another bristle-headed retiree, Nestor, the person for whom Michael had been the substitute. Nestor is carrying ten feet of accordion hose inside a black plastic trash bag. Michael is pleased to buy it for ten bucks.

///

The next morning, they are planning to travel to Morelia, about a hundred and fifty miles away, halfway to Mexico City. It will be a short day, so they are in no hurry to get started. They are about to take Hannah to burn off energy at the pool before the drive, when Dean calls to them from outside the trailer.

"I think you guys should go on ahead without me," he says. Remus, tail slowly wagging, stands at his side.

Michael steps onto the ground, followed by Karen and Hannah.

"What's up?" asks Michael.

"I'm going to stay here in Guadalajara awhile longer. Some guys, ex-Army, like me, they want to take me around Guadalajara with them. It should be fun. I know y'all want to spend some time in Mexico City, but I'm not really up for that. So I'm going to spend a couple more days here then head straight for Oaxaca."

"That's fine. Whatever you want," Michael says. Despite his doubts, Michael likes the cowboy. "But I'm sorry. It's been good traveling with you."

Hannah puts her thumb in her mouth.

Karen says, "I'm sorry too. I'm going to miss you."

"I'll catch up to y'all in Oaxaca, at *La Resolana*, right?"

Karen says, "I'll be looking for you."

"Can we stay here, too?" asks Hannah.

"No," Michael says. "We want to see what's in Mexico City, don't we?"

"But Remus," says Hannah, and she starts to cry.

Karen wants to remove Hannah quickly, to take her away from the source of her sadness. She says, "Come on, kiddo. Let's go for that swim." She reaches for Hannah's hand but the child pulls away and steps up into the trailer, crying. Her mother watches the door close.

"We'll be in Oaxaca," says Dean.

Then Michael speaks loudly so that Hannah can hear him, addressing the screen door, "Hannah, don't cry. Remus will be in Oaxaca."

"Is that a promise?" asks Karen, studying Dean.

Dean removes his hat and runs his hand through his hair. "Well, you never know," he says. "But I'm plannin' on it."

After a few minutes spent soothing and reassuring the child, they go to the pool.

The Nameless

From the infinite reaches to the smallest centers of creation there is an ever-changing balance - the nameless constancy of change, The Mystery without a solution. The ultimate conundrum cannot have a name. People give it names anyway, and by so doing make it absurd. We call it something with gender and will, implying that there are reasons, confusing the way with a will. And onto this unknowable, we project what we know, moment by moment.

So what?

Yet, the words... the words... how beautifully they make the world seem. In the right order, properly chosen, they still the moments. Around us, inside us - pull and push, rise and fall, give and take, still and moving, good and evil, little and big - everything is in opposition except the balance.

He must get to Oaxaca. That's his road now, his chosen path on the heavy earth. How much gas is in the tank? How much tread is left on the tires? Where shall we go today. What shall we eat? Go with the flow and ignore the unknowable. He will not worry about finding the middle path - it will find him.

Rage

The enclosed campground in Oaxaca is so nice that it doesn't seem like a campground. Less than a dozen widely-spaced vehicles are hooked-up along a circular, tree-shaded avenue. The whitewashed walls are covered in flowering vines. A jacaranda tree stands in the center of the circle, its thousand blue flowers fallen to the ground like a painted shadow.

Downtown Oaxaca features a market hall to which they can drive in five minutes. The market is near a town square, the *zocalo*, that has whitewashed tree trunks along the pathways and a bandstand in the center where marimba music is played intermittently, mostly in the evenings.

Wherever they go, they are treated with cordial respect. People here are just like people everywhere - keeping safe, making a living, raising children, and so on. They are not primitive, just a little closer to existence, with less technology between them and the stuff of their lives. The Indian culture is more pronounced here than in Mexico's Northern cities. In the USA, culture is based on adapting to the new. Here, it seems to Michael, there is an indigenous permanence. He is frustrated because he doesn't understand the language well enough to talk to the people about their ideas, having to satisfy himself with impressions.

Oaxaca is as modern as it has to be. There are television sets scattered around the market and visible through open doorways on the streets of the city. There are cars aplenty, as Oaxaca is a venerable university town with a major teaching hospital. Jet planes fly regularly between Mexico City and a jet airport in the broad valley nearby.

They have been here for a few weeks now. Michael has been on the lookout for business opportunities, looking for inexpensive goods of fine quality that he can resell at a profit. Karen is fascinated by the products as objects, by the craftsmanship and attractiveness of the wares and garments made by hand in the valleys surrounding the ancient city.

Hannah participates in the enthusiasms of her parents, happy to look at this and that, to see whatever they point out to her as worthy of attention. She likes the market's candy aisle best, and a lot of places sell toys. Sometimes Mommy and Daddy both take her to the market. Mostly it's just her and Daddy.

They don't buy much. There isn't space in their traveling cube for anything new, as every nook and cranny is already filled with the necessities of their nomadic life. They are wearing locally-made clothing now, sandals of woven leather strips, thin cotton shirts, and embroidered dresses. They walk the aisles of the hall on daily shopping trips, trying not to appear conspicuously *gringo*, learning where the stalls are located and how much things

cost, enjoying the bustle of a community that has flour-
ished for centuries.

Every few days, as today, they take long rides in the
car to visit the villages where the embroidery, rugs, pottery, sandals, hammocks, and whatnots are made. Today
they intend to visit the remnants of a pre-Columbian city
of stone pyramids and foundations, Monte Albán, on a
nearby mountaintop.

They are getting into the car, all ready to go. After she
makes sure Hannah is buckled onto the back seat, Karen
says, "You know what? I don't feel like walking around
any ruins today. I'll stay here."

Michael says, "What's going on?"

"Nothing. Just go ahead without me."

"Why? What's going on?"

"Just go without me, alright. You're all packed up and
ready. You don't need me. Just go on."

"What the hell? Karen? What's up?"

"Nothing."

"So what are you going to do? Just sit around when
you could be with us? What's going on?"

"I just decided that I don't feel like it. All right? I'm
fine. Nothing's going on. I'll be here when you get back."
She closes the door to the backseat and goes into the
trailer without a backward glance.

So they leave her at *La Resolana* and drive out of the
city. Hannah sucking her thumb, Michael, pondering

Karen's behavior, too preoccupied to comment on the sights they pass in his usual tour guide manner. Goddam her! He is angry, with a primitive rage in his guts that he's not felt since his childhood.

They walk around the ruins of Monte Albán, the bones of a vanished civilization. They watch a passenger plane from Mexico City slow in the light mountain air, glide to the runway in the valley below, and land gracefully.

Karen, as ever, is as vague as fog. She has been reluctant to spend time with him, preoccupied with her chores, her books, or with other Americans at the campground. But that's not new. What's changed is that she's been excusing herself from sex, bringing her nothingness to their bed. It used to be that she was most real to him when they were making love. Now, it's as if she's disappearing.

He needs sex with his wife like an infant needs a mother's teat. He relies on her willingness, and his annoyance over her dereliction of wifely duty is yet another stream flowing into his lake of angry waters.

It's Dean, he's pretty sure. Karen tries not to show it, but she has a thing for him. She primps before she and Hannah go with Dean on his hour-long walks with the dog on the streets outside the campground gate. Of late, she urges him to take Hannah on their forays while she stays behind. She's fucking him!

"Come on," he says to Hannah. "Let's see if we can climb to the top of that pyramid."

They walk across the green mountain grass to the ancient stone tiers. Hannah clambers up each one, Michael right behind her as she ascends, to catch her in case she falls.

It's humiliating. They are making a fool of him. Goddam the both off them!

How could she do this to Hannah? What will the poor child do without her mother? Without him? And Dean is a man who demands instant obedience, not the sort he wants anywhere near his daughter.

"Are you tired?" he asks. "We don't have to get to the top."

"No, I'm not tired. I like climbing."

"All right," he says. "But let's be careful."

At the top of the pyramid, the highest point of the mountaintop, the ancients had built a square stone room. They rest with their backs to its outer wall, looking across the valley to the city miles away.

"Don't suck your thumb," he says, and she removes it from her mouth.

Karen frustrates him. He can't reason with her about their situation because she won't engage with him. Save for her care for Hannah, she's a vacuum.

So maybe this it. Maybe the situation is finally coming to a head. How often has he fantasized of being rid of her? Perhaps, instead of anger, he should be peaceful. But his jealous anger is real and powerful, beyond the reach of reason.

If Only

Karen is lying beside Dean in the capacious bed of his *Winnebago*. It is a mild afternoon, the air scented by the flowers of the garden. "I can't keep this up," Karen says.

"He knows?"

His body, long curves and smooth muscle, is beautiful to her. She studies it compulsively, unable to look away from the tendons of his feet or the line of his jaw.

She says, "He's getting angry. I can't keep this up."

"So what are you going to do?"

"I'm asking you. What am I going to do? Do you want to end us?"

"I'd rather not. But if that's how it has to be… ."

"Will you take us in?"

"I've thought about it," he says. "I can't. Not now."

"You're married, aren't you?"

"No. Absolutely not. But I have… commitments."

She hasn't, until now, a month after he'd shown up at Catch-22, mentioned her suspicions. Since then, whenever she can manage it, she comes to the *Winnebago* to make love. Why spoil these delicious interludes of dangerous joy with too much knowledge?

"You're still in the Army, aren't you?"

"Listen. I didn't mean for any of this to happen. You and me, we are an accident that turned out to be something else. But I move around a lot, I'm supposed to be on my own."

She says. "I can keep your secrets."

"But you're not allowed to know... anything. No one is. But why does it have to end? If he doesn't know, why tell him?"

"Because I can't keep on pretending. It's too hard. I think he already suspects that something is going on. We almost had a fight about it this morning."

That first afternoon at Catch-22, it *had* seemed accidental. She had been alone, momentarily liberated from her wife and mother self, and his desire for her had been apparent from the moment they'd said hello on the packed earth behind the dune. The lust had overcome her like a storm, as if their lovemaking had been destined, unavoidable. They had done it because they had to. It had been right, and it had felt right every time since.

He keeps secrets; she doesn't really know who he is. That time in Culiacan, when Michael had gone off on an errand, the first time the Baumgartners had offered to mind Hannah, he'd put some papers away as she'd stepped inside his arvee. And on another occasion, he'd warned her that he was expecting a visitor and that she should therefore keep away from the *Winnebago*. Then, he'd stayed behind in Guadalajara with some ex-Army people from the campground, a place that was like an Army base. Here in Oaxaca, the friend to whom he was supposed to deliver the *Winnebago* hasn't materialized, and Dean dismisses his absence as unimportant. He goes away from the Oaxaca campground for hours at a time, leaving Remus to guard the arvee, and says only that he's got people to meet. She wants to know his secrets, but knows that knowing might ruin their relationship.

The fantasy of moving in with him has been hardening in her imagination. When it had first occurred to her, it had seemed a silly notion. But since then, with each visit to his bed, the need to fix their roles in her understanding has grown greater. Who is she to him? Who is he? What is she doing, behaving in this way? If she were to move in with him − with Hannah, of course − it would prove the rightness of her behavior and validate the depth of her love. If he was to take them in, it would be perfect, it would solve everything.

 "I'm in love with you," she says.

"I know."

"And you love me?"

"Yes, damn it,"

"Doesn't that come first?"

"It means a lot… it does. This has all been so great… you and me. But I have to do some things and I can't be worrying about you and Hannah. It's too bad you have to tell him."

"I have to. It's too hard not to. You mean so much to me that I have to confess it. I am in love with you and don't want to feel ashamed of it."

"Please don't tell him yet."

"What do you mean by 'yet'? What's going to change?"

"I'm leaving for awhile. When I come back... if everything goes okay where I'm going... we'll see. Things should be different. But I have to do this thing first. So try not to tell him until I get back."

She rolls into him, holds him tighter. "When are you leaving?"

"Early tomorrow morning. What do you think Michael will say when you tell him?"

"I don't know. I really don't. He might be glad."

"Glad? I don't think so."

"I've told you. We're not in love anymore. He wants to get rid of me."

"I don't think you get it," says Dean. "He's a man. Men get angry."

"I've never seen him lose his temper," she says. "His feelings will be hurt, at first. He might get upset, he might not. I never know what he's going to do. But if you'll take us in, then we won't have to deal with it."

"I'll be going back to the States soon."

"Take us with you. It would be so wonderful."

"You don't know anything about me. How do you know it would be wonderful?"

"I just know," she says. "This thing you have to do… is it dangerous?"

"Naah. All in a day's work."

"What work? What do you do?"

"Please, don't worry about it."

"So long as you promise to come back, I won't. How long will you be gone?"

"A week or so."

"I suppose I can hold off that long."

"That would be the right thing to do."

The Truth

That night, after Hannah falls asleep, Michael asks Karen to step outside the trailer with him.

"I don't know what's going on with you," he says. "Tell me what's happening. I need to know why you have been acting so strange."

"I didn't realize that I was acting strange. What do you mean?"

"You know," he says.

"No, I don't."

"Like, how come you don't want us to have sex anymore?"

"I haven't felt like it, that's all."

"Just like that? All of a sudden you don't want to do it with your husband? You're telling me it just happened? I don't understand that. Are you having an affair?"

"What? We live in a goddam trailer in the middle of Mexico! How the hell could I manage that? You're crazy."

"You and Dean… You're … You're doing it, aren't you?"

"I can't talk to you. You're crazy. You've finally gone off the deep end."

"Me? I'm not the one acting crazy. It's you! It's like you've disappeared on me. You've changed,"

"I just don't feel like it. That's all."

"You aren't sick, so what's wrong?"

She takes a long moment to answer. "Maybe I'm sick of you," she says. "You talk about feeling ignored? You don't talk to me either. Maybe I'm just tired of being ignored."

"I ignore you?"

"Unless it's for sex, yeah. I'm tired of it. Sick of it."

"I don't mean to ignore you. How can I ignore you? You're right here. I talk to you."

"You talk to Hannah. It's as if I'm not even here."

"You're mad at me because I talk to Hannah?" he says.

"That's not what I said. It's not because you talk to Hannah. See how you just twisted what I said? That's what you always do. What's the point of talking to you? You turn everything I say around and make it into a lecture, so I've stopped bothering. And a lot of the time, you don't hear me when I *do* say something. *I* ignore *you*?! That's a laugh. But I wouldn't say I'm mad at you... just sick and tired of you; of all your talk talk talk and all your dreamy trances and your... just you! Maybe I'm tired of worrying about our future. Maybe I've finally had enough. I'm just sick and tired of it, that's all, sick and tired of you."

"But I thought you just said I don't talk to you. Now you say I talk too much. Which is it?"

"You just did it again! You twist everything. Talking to you just gives you a chance to disagree, to make an argument. You talk with Hannah and everybody else all the time, but with me it's always an argument."

She had bought a pretty shawl made of soft blue, red, and purple yarn at *El Mercado Benito Juarez*. She pulls it tight around her shoulders and turns away from him to reenter the trailer.

"Don't just walk away! We have to talk."

"Right now, I'm going inside."

"What about Dean?"

"What about him?"

"Are you having an affair with him?"

She stands still and turns to face him. "Yes. Yes I am," she says

Like lava, anger rises inside him. He inhales deeply, fills his chest, raises his shoulders. "I knew it."

"I thought you did. I was going to tell you soon, maybe even tonight, if you hadn't started it."

"Jesus! How could you do this?"

"I couldn't help it. It was like it was meant to happen. I just did it."

"It was your choice to make!"

"It didn't feel as if I had a choice. Michael, this isn't about you. For once, it's not about your tortured soul. Okay? This is about me. About my needs."

"You need *him*? No, you need *me*! How can you get along without *me*?"

"I know," she says. "I've gone crazy. I'm nuts. So, we stop having sex. Otherwise, we all get along just fine. Hannah needs you. Only one thing has to change."

"But that changes everything. Now who's delusional?"

"That's your choice, isn't it? You can just keep on like we always do, or you can go all angry husband on me. That's up to you."

"What about me? I need you."

"All you need is my body and I've decided that you can't have it. It's mine."

"But we're married. You promised."

"I know. And I want to stay married, for Hannah's sake."

"What's a marriage without sex?"

"I guess we're about to find out."

"I'm going to go talk to Dean," he says.

"And what? Punch him in the face?"

"Exactly!"

"Please don't do that. Stop and think."

Dean's site is on the opposite side of the circle. Michael spins away and hurries across the campground, Karen on his heels, through the dark moonshade under the jacaranda tree.

"Michael. Michael. Stop!"

He lengthens his stride. She runs to keep up, passes him, and reaches the door of Dean's *Winnebago* ahead of him, and stands with her back to it. The rage boils over; he grips one of her arms with both hands and shoves her to the side. The dog barks, and Dean appears behind the screen door. Karen grabs Michael's sleeve and tries to pull him away.

"You son of a bitch! You goddam son of a bitch!" Michael says.

"Remus. No!" says Dean.

The dog's bark becomes a growl.

Michael reaches for the door handle, but it's locked.

"Let me in!" he demands.

"Whoa! Slow down," says Dean.

"Come out here! Come out here so I can get my hands on you, you bastard."

"Michael! Stop this! Please," says Karen.

"The two of you! You fuckers!"

She's managed to get herself between him and the door again, and she pushes him backward. "Go away," she says. "You're acting crazy. Just go."

He takes her by the shoulders and tosses her aside so forcefully that she falls to the ground. The dog starts barking again.

Karen, unhurt, gets to her feet. "You bastard!" she says.

The commotion has attracted the attention of other campground residents, including the couple occupying the pickup camper in the next-over space, who stand a dozen paces away, warily watching the spectacle.

Furious, he makes a fist and pulls it to his shoulder, about to punch her. The image of The Tao, ☯, the embracing teardrops of serenity, flickers in his mind.

The Baumgartners, Gloria and Vic, with their dachshunds, are approaching from farther around the avenue. The door of another trailer opens, spilling electric light into the gloom.

Dean Scanlon stands inside his gigantic arvee with his barking dog. "Remus! No!" he says.

When the dog stops, in the sudden silence, Michael hears faint notes of the distant marimbas.

His anger is overflowing, his raised arm feels like a steam-powered piston. The Tao starts to spin, and he wills it still.

"Bastard! You pushed me!" says Karen.

Be still. Be still. The anger is the juice of him.

"What is the matter with you? You're nuts," she says.

Breathe. And again. Hush… sh. Still… Be still.

He turns away.

On the return walk under the tree, the fallen petals mute the sound of his footsteps. He stops at the car and turns to look back at the Winnebago. Dean is in the doorway, closing the outer door. Michael lights a cigarette to settle his nerves, never taking his eyes from the *Winnebago*.

Hannah is sleeping when he goes inside. In the dark, he stands to look at his daughter's peaceful face, then sits on the sofa bench, facing the table under Hannah's bunk, the table that collapses to form the bed where he and Karen sleep. If he were to sleep alone tonight, it would be the first time in…? How long? They have been married for seven years.

Will she come back? He has made her afraid of him. And, as he assesses the trembling anger in his guts, he doesn't trust himself. She is making him crazy. It would be better if she didn't come back. But Karen won't spend a night away from her child; so, she'll be back.

Should he lock the door? No.

He slides out the shelf that extends from under the sofa and uses the back cushions to complete the mattress for the trailer's third bed, retrieves bedding from the bin under the dining bench, and prepares to sleep alone.

Is she with Dean now, at this very moment? It is so wrong that he cannot conjure an image of it. Karen is *his*; she *cannot* be with someone else; they are *married*; it is *wrong*. He has been wronged. Poor him. Oh, the pity.

That's pretty funny, and he smiles.

Knots

Dean Scanlon unlocks the door, takes Karen by the hand, walks her inside, closes the outer door, gets her seated at his table, turns down the lights, and says, "Wow. He's really pissed off."

Karen says, "He just picked me up and threw me! He really scared me. What should I do?"

"You think he's going to hurt you?"

"I think he wants to. I have to get Hannah."

"You should let him cool off for a few minutes. I mean, right now, he's nuts."

"He might hurt her," she says. "Do you think he'll hurt her?"

"Why would he do that?"

"I don't know," she says. "It's just that I don't recognize him. He's so angry!"

"But he's Michael; he wouldn't hurt anyone, let alone his own daughter. I'm sure she's safe with him."

Tears spill from her eyes and down her cheeks and her nose starts to run and… and she's sobbing like a child. Dean hands her a tissue box.

"This is really bad. I have to get back," she says, rising from the table.

"He's mad at you, not her. Stay for a bit. Let him cool off."

"What if he leaves?"

Dean, looking out a window, says, "We can see your site from here. If he starts to move out, we can stop him at the gate.

"Do you see Michael?"

"Yes. He's having a smoke. Come look."

Their site is about fifty feet away, close enough to a lamppost that she can see Michael leaning against the car. Their trailer, farther back from the quiet street, in the shadows, is dark. Hannah, she hopes, is still asleep.

"I didn't bring my cigarettes," she says, taking a *Marlboro* from the pack on the table as she sits down. Her hand trembles as she lights up. "How long do you think I should wait?"

"As long as possible," says Dean. "He'll cool down. I thought you weren't going to tell him."

"He brought it up. He'd already guessed it. I couldn't deny it."

"So what are you going to do?"

"Do? I guess I go back to Hannah and hope for the best. There's nothing I can do but deal with him. He knows, so I have to see what he's going to do about it. I really didn't think he would be this upset."

"I think we have both been a little bit nuts. Me too. I didn't want to think about what Michael was going to do," he says. "It's not all your fault."

She raises her head and looks him in the face. Managing a slight smile, she says, "Well, that's nice of you to say. But, what difference does that make? You don't have to live with him... I do."

"That's going to be really hard for you. I'm sorry."

"Well, there's no point to being sorry. I knew what I was doing. I want you, need you. I still do," she says, blows her nose, and takes another drag of the cigarette.

"Yeah. I guess this is the price, " he says. He sits down across from her, reaches forward, puts his hand under her chin and strokes her jaw with his thumb. "I hate to see you so sad."

"I'll make us some tea," she says.

She busies herself at Dean's sink and stove, brings mugs and teabags out of the cupboard, waits for the water to boil, checks out the window, sees Michael go inside their little trailer, fills the mugs, and places them on the table with a spoon and a jar of honey.

"You're sure we can't come with you in the morning?" she asks.

"Not possible. I'm sorry." He strokes her cheek and runs his fingers through the hair on her temple.

"Stop it. Please. Don't touch me."

He takes his hand away and crosses his forearms on the table. He had turned off all but a weak light by the closed door to his bedroom, a low-wattage bulb in a

207

frosted glass sconce that casts a sideways light on them as they face each other. It is quiet outside.

"I'm sorry," she says. "You can't touch me. We have to stop."

"Okay," he says.

"This is over. Right now."

"Yes, I guess it is," he says, then, "See? I told you he'd be mad."

"Maybe he'll get over it."

"Maybe he will."

"What's going to happen when you come back from your job?"

"I don't know. I guess that will be up to us," he says.

"So Hannah and I could be part of the plan."

"I have to do this job, and I don't have any plans for after."

"Will you keep the *Winnebago*?"

"I'll be allowed to keep it until I quit."

"Do you have a house in Texas?"

"Nothing permanent," he says.

She gets up from the table and looks across to their unlit trailer. Her husband and her daughter are over there, where she belongs.

"I think I can go back now," she says.

She turns the handle on the outer door, opens it, and stands there, reluctant to leave. He rises and comes to her.

She closes the door. He wraps her in his embrace and they kiss. She pulls away, opens the door, and leaves him.

She walks across the middle of the circle to their site, hesitates, opens the door, and steps up to their darkened cube. Michael, lying in the sofa bed, sits up, and whispers, "I'm sleeping here tonight."

She unlatches the table leg, forms the platform for her mattress, removes her nightgown and the bedding from the bin, and makes up her bed. In the bathroom, she gets out of her clothes and puts on the nightgown. For the first time in seven years, she will sleep alone.

And so they lie silently through the night. As a rooster crows, they both fall asleep. Shortly thereafter, she opens her eyes when the *Winnebago's* engine starts up. Faint daylight comes through the windows. She hears huge tires on the pavement. She falls back asleep as roosters from all the surrounding yards declare their territory.

PART THREE

The Superior Man

Learning the truth about Karen and Dean has changed Michael. He'd come close to violence, his anger like steam inside a cylinder. For a clarifying instant, feeling like a weapon, with his fist raised at his wife's terrified face, he had imagined the symbol of *Tao*. He'd lowered his fist, and turned away. That had been a week ago. Since that night, he has focused his attention on *The I Ching*.

He is resonating with the times, 1973 being a year when cults are proliferating, astrology is having a renaissance, Christians are being born again, the spirit gods are being discovered in drumbeats and sweat lodges, The Beatles have a guru, and psychics practice on California cliff tops. Too, he's on the road in Mexico, living amongst vagabonds who tend to be proudly nonconformist. Whatever the reasons, his spiritual sensitivity has been awakened, as if he's suffered a blow to the head. What he doesn't consider is that he is heartbroken. In his tender condition, the ancient sentences of *The I Ching* seem profoundly wise.

Dean has gone. Michael has not seen him since that evening, when he'd been standing in the doorway of his *Winnebago*, next to his big, black dog. Since Dean left, his large site has been occupied by a couple from Baltimore who live in an arvee of similar, great dimensions. Michael assumes that Dean chose to remove himself from a messy affair before things got worse. Had he been Dean Scanlon, that's what he would have done, as would any reasonable man.

Michael and Karen avoid the confinement of the trailer unless it's mealtime, or bedtime, or fold the laundry time. He takes Hannah with him on trips to town, or Karen does. When the three of them are together, they talk about the food, the weather, or the latest arrival at *La Resolana.* When Hannah is asleep, they take to their separate beds.

The child seems unaware, and that's as it should be.

Karen is placid and unemotional, distant and receding.

But he doesn't mind. In fact, he welcomes her lack of attention to him, as it frees him to go even deeper into the mysteries. Her affair proves that she recognizes that the marriage is doomed, and that's a very good thing. She has finally asserted herself. This is a great accomplishment, as it has been her passive acceptance of his choices, as much as his attempts to extricate himself, that have brought them to their current circumstances. Now, at last, they might be free of each other. When their wounds heal, they will talk about it.

Karen is at the sink, rinsing apples. She sets apples on a dish towel to dry, and says, "We're going into town and look around. What do you say, kiddo? Shall we go find you a sweater?"

"And it's Saturday," Michael says. "Give them my best." Saturday mornings are when she calls her parents in Philadelphia, without fail.

And so he is left in blessed solitude with *The I Ching, The Book of Change,* by Anonymous. He dislikes the idea of religion. He has read about the "great" religions, and considers all of them mistakes. It's not that he knows better – he doesn't know anything at all. But he hasn't read or heard anything that he can believe in more than what he can reason for himself.

No one knows who wrote *The I Ching* or exactly how old it is. The translator of his copy speculates that it's been in use for over three thousand years, written in biblical times, when China was a great empire. It seems to have been meant as guidance to men in positions of power and influence in the far flung dominions. Rather than a book of instructions, or a rule book, or a policy manual, it was intended as a method of reasoning that could be applied to each unique situation as it occurred, a way of choosing the best options in any circumstances. As such, it is necessarily abstract, so generalized that it can be consulted to help anyone reason through any sort of dilemma. In this sense, it is like a bible. But, unlike the Judeo Christian bible, it is without a saga, and The Divine is not described as an all-powerful being with a will, like a person, but as the uncaring change of the universe.

The Book of Change describes the behavior of an archetype, a "Superior Man," a sort of a Taoist saint, a person so wise that he is always at peace, always admired, always successful, always righteous. The Superior Man is a humble, quiet person who seeks harmony with Man and Nature, one who avoids harm and acts only to achieve good results. Accordingly, a person searching for The Way, *Tao*, the good and balanced life, emulates such a person. There is much in the *I Ching* that he finds baffling and irrelevant, but not The Superior Man.

The I Ching, for those who value it, satisfies the need to make sense of what's always in process. The book's fundamental idea is that any situation, no matter how complex and dynamic, can be frozen and analyzed. It's a method of halting change, of stopping time. Science is based on the same conceit, and so is Art.

Michael rejects the magical claims of *The I Ching*. He does not believe that some mysterious force arranges coins to land one way or another. Therefore, anything assumed by their arrangement is false, because a connection between random events and one of sixty-four chapters in a book is logically impossible. Because the way the coins settle is accidental, any relationship between a set of heads or tails and the description of an ancient diagram is preposterous.

Yet, he keeps reading the book, picking hexagrams at random, asking himself questions.

Each hexagram seems a perfect design, reassuring in its simplicity. At the most superficial level, simply as sixty-four unique arrangements of lines and dashes, the *I Ching's* drawings are balanced and pleasing to look at. He opens pages at random just to stare at the hypnotic arrangements.

Hexagram 10   Hexagram 21   Hexagram 45

As for the texts, if he ignores the ambiguities and the nonsense, he can make the *I Ching* seem to work. With minimal creative reasoning, he's able to tease some kind of sense out of what's written as an answer to any question he poses.

The book is written as guidance for The Superior Man. It contains hundreds of references to this paragon – a person who eschews ambition and riches, who succeeds in his endeavors, and is admired by everyone. He enjoys inner peace because he is virtuous, avoiding harmful acts, attempting to make things better with every word and deed. His virtue is its own reward, the source of his tranquility. According to this circular logic, if Michael acts like a Superior Man, any path he chooses will, *ipso facto,* be the right one. The book, therefore, is not only about what to do; it is also about who to be.

Michael does not think he's superior, he's not even exceptional. His height, weight, and coloring are exactly the average for an American man of his age. He had never excelled at school or on playgrounds. He's never won awards. He has few friends and is seldom invited to parties. He's ordinary. But if he imitates the behavior of a Superior Man, the consequences of his choices will be as positive as possible.

The Superior Man's great challenge is to restrain himself. His instincts, as a man, are always to *do* something. He enjoys beneficial results by regulating his powers, doing as little as necessary, conscious that doing nothing has as much positive potential as action. And, if there is a Superior Man, there is necessarily a Superior Woman, a person who is challenged to overcome her instinct to let things be. Both seek internal balance, a manifestation of *Tao.* A family, as an entity unto itself, is not adjusted unless the man and woman as individuals have found internal equilibrium.

The I Ching claims itself oracular, able to divine the future, but cautions that the likelihood of getting this benefit is proportional to a person's seriousness of purpose. A Superior Woman or Man is insignificant, possessed of imagination too tiny to comprehend all of the forces and balances of Creation, but whose humility and sense of wonder make them receptive to the magic of the book.

What if, as nonsensical as that seems, it's true? What if Michael's future will be revealed to him! In his fragile mental state, he has convinced himself that, if he asks the question in the right way, he might be shown a blinding truth. But he has yet to write the question down or toss the coins. In preparation, he has been testing the book and his ability to take its meaning, forming questions in his mind and consulting pages at random. The translator who'd written the introduction to his copy recommends just this sort of training.

Each hexagram has a unique name, sort of a metaphor that summarizes the overarching meaning. The fuller meanings of the hexagrams are intricately complicated, as they were written according to a strict, multi-layered methodology. The three-line combinations, the *trigrams*, of which there are four in each stack − the bottom three, the top three, the 5th, 4th and 3rd lines from the bottom, and the 4th, 3rd and 2nd − have meaning in the context of the other three.

At the lowest level of description are the lines, each meaning dependent on whether a line is adjacent to another of its kind or to its opposite, or whether it is above or below, or whether it is on the top or the bottom of the stack, or where it fits in a trigram. Representing inaction, femininity, and passivity, *Yin* lines, are drawn as _____

_____ . *Yang* lines, representing action, masculinity, making-something-happen, are drawn _____ . The lines are meaningless absent an understanding of their opposites: movement can only be understood as 'not stillness', emptiness as 'not fullness', increase as 'not decrease', and so on.

Now, while Karen and Hannah are out shopping for sweaters, he asks whether the time has come to conclude the Mexican odyssey and return to the States to look for employment.

With his eyes closed, he opens the book to

Hexagram 44
"KOU"
CONTACT (SEXUAL
INTERCOURSE, MEETING, Etc.)

Sex! That's interesting. Why not?

The text for the bottom line, the only *yin*, or female line, in the hexagram, reads. *"The chariot wheel is held with a metal brake. Persistence in a righteous course brings good fortune. Those with an objective in view will witness misfortune. However, even a lean pig is able to wiggle its trotters. COMMENTARY: The first sentence implies that the weak have to be dragged."*

For the next to last line, the lowest of the five active *yang* lines, *"There is fish in the bag – no error! But it is of no advantage to our guests. COMMENTARY: This implies that we are not dutiful to our guests."*

Clichés, obscure metaphors, and poetic abstractions. Nonsense.

Yet, he can make the text fit his circumstances. "Fish in the bag" is congratulatory, "no error." Good for me, the trailer and its occupants are in good shape, thanks to me. They have no guests, so that line is probably irrelevant. As for the bottom line, the female line, Karen and Hannah are like caliper brakes on his wheel, keeping him from moving. But he shouldn't worry about them if he brings them along - they will be okay, their trotters will continue to wiggle.

The first line of text, that "persistence in a righteous course brings good fortune," causes him difficulty, because he doubts that pursuing a teaching job is the correct course. And even if he consciously dedicates himself to that end, "with his objective in view," he will witness misfortune.

The name of the hexagram baffles him. "KOU" suggests that the problem should be addressed with copulation in mind. Well, he's a man. So maybe the predominance of unbroken lines means that going home is a manly, aggressive choice. Or maybe it simply means that he is driven by sex. That's it! All of this is about having a better sex life! There's a lot of truth in that.

Or maybe it means the opposite; that he should ignore sex completely. This could be the case depending on whether, if he was actually to throw the coins, two or three heads or tails were the result of a toss. Three of a kind would mean that the line is mature, at the end of its cycle of transformations, and morphing into its opposite. Thus there is a second hexagram, equally as confusing, to be consulted for any set of results. In these secondary hexagrams, mature *yang* lines are _____o_____ and mature *yin* lines are _____x_____.

He looks at some of the other hexagrams, each with declarations about The Superior Man. *Hexagram 10, "The Superior Man may go without food for three days on end, so intent is he on reaching his goal." Hexagram 23, "The Superior Man respectfully contemplates the ebb and flow, the unending succession of repetition and depletion which constitutes the way of heaven."*

His writing talent, if he has any, is unproven. Without genius, he would have to dedicate his entire being to so exalted an objective. It would be enormously difficult, perhaps impossible for someone with his meager gifts. He would have to devote himself to it, his pursuit single-minded and selfish, requiring him to put the task before everything else, even his family. That doesn't seem right-eous. Should he do it anyway? Can he do it? When? Will he? How? Which path is righteous?

He has not framed a question about what he cares most about, because he is afraid of the truth. He has not written it down. He has not tossed three coins six times. He does not want to be told that he has no chance of be-coming an author. He will ask once and be done with it. If the *I Ching's* answer turns out to be nonsense, he will have lost nothing.

Touching Base

Karen soaks fruits and vegetables in a light bleach solution for an hour or so after she brings them back from the market. She keeps the dishpan she uses for the purpose on the picnic table outside their trailer door. At *La Resolana*, a truck loaded with the five gallon bottles of *Agua Pura* makes daily deliveries. After an hour or so, she brings the produce inside and rinses it with clean water. They've been in Mexico since early September, it's now late December, and no one has gotten sick.

Today she bought apples. She is rinsing them off at her tiny sink. Michael is in his favorite spot, on the sofa along the back of the trailer, four feet away to her right. At the table to her left, Hannah is finishing a glass of milk and a peanut butter and jelly sandwich. Time to get moving.

She says, "We're going into town and look around for a sweater for Hannah. She needs another one. What do you say, kiddo? Shall we go find you a sweater?"

"And it's Saturday," Michael says. "Give them my best." She calls her parents from a phone booth inside *El Mercado Benito Juarez* every Saturday morning. After she talks to them, they will shop for a sweater. It will be fun.

When Michael had stood above her with his fist raised, his mask of affability blown off by anger, she'd seen the face of a man who hated her. Then he'd stepped back, lowered his arm, gotten a distracted look on his face, as if he was listening to something, turned, and walked away. That had been three nights ago, and she is still processing the idea that her husband hates her.

She does not expect to see Dean again. At first, she'd watched the gates of *La Resolana*, hoping to see him returning. Then she'd stopped waiting, dismissing the prospect as fantasy.

Dean had been too good to be true, as if she'd made him up in a dream while dozing on a sand dune on a sunny afternoon. He didn't used to be in her life, and he isn't going to be. He'd been a chapter, a scene, a fantasy. It's over. It had been too intense to have lasted - over because it had to end. It had been so sudden, the ending as abrupt as the beginning. And that makes it easier for her to tuck the affair into one of the places where she keeps her secrets. She will forget about it. It had been great while it lasted.

Michael has been strange since that night, the night he'd thrown her on the ground, ready to kill her. But since then... nothing. He's been super nice, even cheerful, as if he's happy that she'd fallen in love with somebody else. Maybe he is. Or maybe it's because of that stupid book he keeps reading. My God, how long can a person read one book? Whatever, she prefers this version of Michael. He's content to sit and read, a polite companion, a cheerful neighbor to the other residents of *La Resolana*, a doting father. He scarcely acknowledges their departure for *El Mercado Benito Juarez*, so absorbed is he in that Chinese book.

She aches, down deep, far enough down that she can act as if the pain isn't there. But wouldn't it be grand to see Dean's great big *Winnebago* rolling back into her life! She feels disappointment, as if, in spite of herself, she expects to see him driving through the gates as she and Hanna leave for the market. The clear nights are chilly in the mountains, and the little girl has outgrown the sweater she's been wearing.

Hannah says, "I think we should have a dog."

"You do, do you?"

"Yes, I do."

"There's not enough room for a dog in the trailer."

"We could get a little puppy."

"No, we could not. They poop and pee on everything. Can you imagine that in our itsy bitsy trailer? No way."

"Can we have a cat?"

"We've been through this before. I have told you a hundred times, I am allergic to cats."

"For ever?" Hannah asks.

"Yes. Forever. That's the way it is, kiddo. You'll have to wait until you grow up."

"That's not fair. Other kids have a pet."

"Sorry."

"Their Mommies aren't allergic. Why are you?"

"What color sweater are you looking for?"

"Daddy wants a dog."

"No he doesn't."

"Yes he does. Daddy loves dogs. I bet he wants a dog. A puppy."

"I think we should get you a really nice sweater. The ladies down here knit them by hand."

"I don't want a sweater. I want a dog."

"Enough! We're not going to talk about it anymore."

Predictably, Hannah puts her thumb in her mouth.

She parks the car on the street, a block from the *Zócalo*, the town square. They walk to the market, a high-ceilinged space inside a block square building where hundreds of venders sell their goods. The phone booths are near the entrance.

She has mastered enough Spanish to ask the operator for a long distance, collect call to her parents' home in Cheltenham, a Philadelphia suburb. Her father picks up the phone on the first ring.

"Hi, Dad. It's me. And Hannah."

"Hey. Hello," says Mort Curtin.

"I'm on the other phone," says her mother, Terri Curtin. "How are things?"

"Fine. Everything is fine. Terrific."

"So what have you been up to?" her father asks.

"Nothing much," she says. "We take trips with the car a lot. We go looking at blankets and pottery and jewelry and clothes with hand sewn embroidery. Some of this stuff is really beautiful. You'll see. We're bringing back lots of beautiful things."

Her father asks, as he does every time they talk, "And do you have any idea when that's going to happen?"

"No, Dad. I don't."

We are the only chicks Mort and Terri Curtin have ever had in their nest, and we have gone away.

"You can't wait too long," says her mother. "Hannah has to have a residence when she starts kindergarten."

"I know, Mom. We have plenty of time."

"In Cheltenham, you have to have an address for three months in order to be a resident."

Elkins Park, where they had lived, is also in Cheltenham, the same township where the belongings from their apartment are stored. She intends to return to Cheltenham, with or without Michael.

"You have to be back by June. You'll use our address. You'll stay with us," her father says.

"Until we get our own place."

"Don't worry about that. Use our house."

"We'll stay at your house if we have to. We just have to see what happens," Karen says.

"Is Michael all right?"

"Michael's fine. Better than ever."

"Let us talk to Hannah," says her mother.

Karen hands the phone to her daughter. "Hi Grammy," she says. "Hi Grampa. If we stay at your house, can I have a puppy?"

"Give me that," says Karen, and takes the phone back.

"That's her thing at the moment," says Karen. "A dog. She wants a dog."

"Well," says her mother, "That's normal."

"I suppose it is."

"Christmas isn't going to be the same this year," her father says.

"It's pretty amazing down here," she answers. "Mexicans are really into The Church. Holidays are a big deal. They're always having festivals. Believe me, they have Christmas in Mexico."

"Sounds interesting," says her father. "Well, enjoy it. Merry Christmas."

"Merry Christmas, Dad."

"Merry Christmas," says her mother.

"You too, Mom," she says.

A Christmas Surprise

The Baumgartners are hosting a Christmas Eve party, their trailer strung with colored lights. Fresh rolls, plates of sliced meats, condiments, salads, and baked goods are arrayed on tables outside. Beer and *Coke* fill a cooler on the ground. One of the backpackers is plucking tunes vaguely reminiscent of Christmas carols on his guitar.

Michael enjoys the people on the Gringo Trail. They tell him why they are in Oaxaca, where they're from, what they know, what prompted their circumstances. He imagines them as people squeezed out of ripe America: outliers, nonconformists, fugitives.

People respond to Michael's friendly curiosity, his way of asking questions. He is always calm, focused on them, genial, smiling agreement or bemused disagreement, never threatening. He had unconsciously developed these mannerisms in order to critique one-thousand-eight-hundred sophomore speeches without demoralizing the sophomores. But it isn't pretense. He is genuinely curious about everyone, listening for clues about their interests so that he can ask them about what they know.

Jack Doughty lives in a camper atop his pickup truck. He is a seasonal trucker from Alaska who winters in Mexico with a different girl every year. His companion this year is a striking, large-boned woman from Idaho with long, auburn hair called Marissa.

Calvin, the guitarist from the San Fernando Valley who has been hitching rides on his way to Guatemala, is embellishing *Rudolph The Red Nosed Reindeer*. In Calvin's rendering, Rudolph has extremely ugly toes. Calvin hasn't shaved in weeks. He lives in a tent with a girl who is so dazed by the hash oil she dabs with a toothpick onto the insides of cigarette papers before she rolls her joints that she can barely speak. Calvin has not said what his last name is.

The biggest arvee at *La Resolana,* occupying the space where Dean's had been, is owned by people from Baltimore, a longhair named Glenn and his lady, Mina. Mina casts horoscopes. Glenn secretively supervises a marijuana plantation in a mountain valley ten miles from Oaxaca. In preparation for their getaway to Mexico, they had maxed out their credit cards without intending to make payments. If they were to return to the States, they would be arrested for fraud. Glenn is tall and hunched, with a prominent brow shielding wary eyes. He wears a bandana around his head to keep the long hair away from his face. Mina, is a plump, solemn woman with stringy blonde hair who wears dangly earrings and many rings on the fingers of both hands.

Vic and Gloria Baumgartner, the retired couple from Ohio, are one among several couples of similar background, the snowbirds. There are eleven sites with hookups at La Resolana, most occupied by retirees. The backpackers, like Calvin, pitch their small tents on patches at the inside corners of the rectangular grounds. At the moment, thirty-three Americans are residents of *La Resolana*, most living in trailers and arvees parked around the circular avenue with the tree in the middle, and most of them are attending the Christmas party.

Hannah is delighted by Calvin's playing and is sitting on the ground, listening and watching his fingers.

Karen is with two other women, sitting in folding chairs near the door to the Baumgartners' trailer. His conversations with her, since that night, are much the same as they had been before. For Hannah's sake, they are carefully polite. Karen has made friends with several of the women, spending long hours away from the trailer, shopping, cooking, and bonding with her new friends. There are few times when Michael is alone with his wife, and that's fine with him.

Danny Porter and Hortense Brown live in a twenty-five foot trailer whose interior is covered by Mexican weavings and in which books and magazines are in such profusion that one has to clear a space to sit down. Danny is a black man, a jazz musician and composer who suffers from excruciating migraine headaches, the result of a head wound he'd suffered in Korea. They survive on his injured veteran's benefits. Hortense is a white woman who has devoted her life to easing Danny's pain. He ingests copious amounts of garlic to keep the migraine misery in check. Hortense minces garlic to flavor every dish she cooks and keeps jars stuffed with peeled cloves soaking in water for Danny to swallow between meals. Their trailer reeks. Danny reeks, and his eyes are always bloodshot. Danny Porter clearly does not like Calvin's playing and has twice moved his and Hortense's folding chairs to get as far away from the music as he can.

Hortense interests him. She had been a research biologist working at a drug company in New Jersey when Danny convinced her that they'd be better off living in Mexico. What interests him about Hortense is that she studies witchcraft.

Danny's most recent furniture move has brought him and Hortense, as well as their miasma of minced garlic, next to Michael, who stands on the fringe of the party holding a beer and a cigarette.

"You know," Hortense says, "There's such a thing as a witches' Christmas. It's the Winter Solstice. People have been having these parties for a long, long time. It's an ancient festival about fire and light on the shortest day of the year."

"Is that so," says Michael.

"It is," says Hortense Brown. She is a small woman in her forties with gray-streaked hair.

"So what did the witches have to do with it?"

232

"People looked up to the witches before the Catholic Church took over in Europe. They were the ones who understood the mysteries. They ran the holidays. Then it was the Catholic priests instead of the witches. Now it's the scientists, they're the ones who explain the mysteries these days."

"So you're saying witches are like scientists? I thought they were the opposite; you know, believing in magic instead of facts and evidence."

Hortense says, "Scientists do the same things as witches used to do, interpret the unseen and claim to know what makes things happen. Witches used to do exactly that. Not as well, but that was their role."

"Aren't you a scientist?"

"Yes. That too."

"You can be both?"

"I don't practice witchcraft, I read about it. Don't ask me to tell your fortune or cast a spell."

"But you believe in it?"

"I'm interested in how they used natural things in medicine. A lot of healing practices the witches developed over thousands and thousands of years have been forgotten. I think that's too bad. Nowadays, we think anything in a package has magical qualities; we don't look to nature as much as we should."

"Well, that makes sense. Is that where you learned about the garlic?"

"Saved my life," says Danny. "I'd have shot myself without the garlic. When she started making me garlic tea, I was this close to pulling the trigger."

Hortense says, "Doctors have no idea whatsoever about how to treat migraines. They put a name on it, call it 'an ailment', look up the name in a magic book, and find the list of herbs and potions – excuse me, "medicines" – that the sages prescribe, same as the witches used to do. When you're sick, you go to whoever you think can heal you and you pay whatever you can afford. That's people. Now we believe in science. But in their day, the witches were the scientists."

"What about fortune telling?" Michael asks.

Hortense says, "If you believe that spirits control events, and that they can be persuaded, you ask for their help. You pray to them or try to bribe them. If you believe that only certain people can talk to the spirits, then you pay them to do the persuasion, your witches and your priests and your fortune tellers."

"But you wouldn't go to a witch today, would you?"

"Of course I would, so would you, especially if the doctors in their sacred white gowns aren't healing you. Everybody does it."

Mina, the astrologer, whose broad hips testify to her fondness for baked goods, approaches them carrying a tray of cookies. "These are really good, if I do say so myself. I think it's the butter. Have a cookie."

Gloria Baumgartner has been bustling about, keeping things tidy around her campsite. She comes over to sample a cookie.

"Is somebody going to say something to that guy with the guitar?" says Danny.

"Like what?" says Gloria, considering whether to select a cookie with red sprinkles or with green sprinkles.

"Like how about he puts it away or gives it to somebody who knows how to play it."

Calvin is playing something that might be *Oh Tannenbaum.*

Gloria says, "Don't be so scroogey. I think Calvin plays okay. Besides, it's Christmas, it's time to love your fellow man."

"These cookies are great," says Michael.

"I told you," says Mina. "It's the butter down here. Richer."

"So, Mina," says Michael. "We were just talking about fortune tellers."

"Like me," says Mina. "That's what I do."

"I don't understand how you can believe in all that hocus pocus," says Gloria, appreciating a mouthful of cookie.

"Astrology isn't hocus pocus," Mina says. "It's a science. You don't just sit down and cast a horoscope. It takes work to check on all the forces: the stars and planets. You have to know exactly where they're going to be and where they were. And you have to take the constellations and the seasons into account. If that's not science, I don't know what is."

"It's not science," says Hortense. "Come on, Mina, just because you need to use a lot of weird rules doesn't make it scientific."

"They're not weird. You just have to take the time to understand them," Mina answers.

"I'm sure it's not easy, Mina," says Michael. "Where did you get the butter?"

"From the *Super Mercado*, where else?"

"Hey, man," says Calvin, the guitar hanging by a wampum beaded strap across his chest. "Nice party."

"Where'd you learn to play the guitar?" Danny asks.

"I just picked it up," he answers.

Locking eyes with Michael, Gloria says, "Guess who I saw in town today? Dean."

From the meaningful way she looks at Michael, he guesses that she knows about Karen's love affair with the cowboy. She'd observed the spectacle outside the *Winnebago*, and she's been babysitting Hannah for weeks, in regular contact with Karen, who might have confided her secret to the older woman. Or, she might have guessed it by observing Karen's comings and goings.

"Yeah?" says Michael. "Where did you see him?"

"Downtown. He was going into the City Hall."

"Hey. Dean. Cool," says Calvin. He, Michael and Dean had shared a joint a couple of days before the cowboy departed.

"Did you talk to him?" Michael asks.

"No," says Gloria. "I just saw him go in, hat and all. I just thought I'd mention it."

"Who's Dean?" asks Mina.

"He was in your space before you got here. Has a *Winnebago*."

"Well, he's out of luck if he wants the space back," says Mina.

"I'd be surprised if he does," says Michael.

"Hey, Mina, I have an idea," says Danny. "Why don't you ask the stars if Dean's coming back."

Huffily, Mina says, "I could if you could tell me his birthday and where he was born. Otherwise, forget about it."

Michael tilts his head to suggest that Gloria follow him. Out of earshot of the others. He asks, "Did you mention to Karen that you saw Dean?"

"No."

"It may not be such a good idea," he says. "Hannah will go nuts if she thinks she can see Remus again."

Scrutinizing Michael, she says, "I just thought you'd be interested."

"Yeah. Thanks for telling me. But I'd appreciate it if you didn't mention it to Karen."

"Gotcha," says Gloria.

A Stunning Result

On the day after Christmas, Karen goes to the market with Hannah, leaving Michael alone in the trailer. This will be the day he formally consults *The I Ching*, the day his life changes.

He has put aside three, five-centavo coins, shiny brass discs about the size of a dime, with the head of a Mexican heroine embossed on one side, and an eagle killing a snake on the other, heads and tails. He lays a bath towel on the table to keep the coins from rolling after they land. Next to the towel he places *The I Ching*, a notepad, and a pencil that he's sharpened with his pocket knife.

Rituals have been devised as preparation for tossing the coins: reverentially removing the book from its exalted place on a head-high shelf, unfolding the white cloth it's been covered by, using this hand or that hand to turn the pages, burning incense, striking chimes, and so on. He dislikes rituals. Besides, the rituals vary from place to place and have changed over time. They don't have anything to do with the book itself, which hasn't changed in three thousand years. He'll just do it without ritual, trusting that the month he's spent articulating his question and pondering the sayings of Lao Tzu were sufficient preparation. He'll write out the question, toss three coins six times, record the results as a hexagram, and be done with it.

Even though no one is watching, he feels silly and a little embarrassed. It's an experiment, that's all.

At the top of the page, he writes, "Will I be an author?"

He cups the coins between his hands, shakes them up and down, feels them tumble, and allows them to drop onto the towel. Three heads. *Yang*: masculinity, action, doing. He draws ⎯⎯⎯⎯⎯⎯⎯ .

Again – shake, clink-clink, drop. Three heads again. He draws a second unbroken line above the first one.

The third toss is the same.

And so is the fourth.

And so is the fifth.

The sixth toss, despite a few extra shakes, is the same. He finishes the hexagram of six unbroken lines.

All heads, every time! What the hell? Despite his doubts, his cynicism, his rationalism, he is stunned. The likelihood of this result must be exceptionally low. How can this be random? But, if isn't chance, what is it? Destiny?

Hexagram 1
CH'IEN THE CREATIVE PRINCIPLE
lower trigram: heaven male, active, etc.
upper trigram: heaven, male, active, etc.

"Sublime Success! Persistence in a righteous course brings reward."

He scans the text, skipping from sentence to sentence, line to line, too disoriented by the peculiar result to read deeply, finding nothing but encouragement. Wow. He could not have asked for a more positive result. According to the translator, *Ch'ien* is the most significant of all the hexagrams, the touchstone for all the others, it is the most propitious, the one with the least ambiguity, the one that requires the least interpretation, the one that is nothing but positives. Yes, yes, yes - for every line. Yes for each of the trigrams.

But, every single coin had been heads, which is supposed to mean that each line is mature, about to morph into its opposite. The secondary hexagram, therefore, is

Hexagram 2
K'UN THE PASSIVE PRINCIPLE
> *lower trigram: earth, female, passive, etc.*
> *upper trigram: earth, female, passive, etc.*

"Sublime Success! The Superior Man has an objective and sets forth to gain it. At first he goes astray, but later finds his bearings."

He closes the book, pockets the coins, puts away the towel.

The result had been a million-to-one chance, the *guarantee* of success the least likely of all possible results. A million to one shot - and he has the winning ticket. A guarantee! A double guarantee, actually, because the opposite hexagram is equally propitious. Whether he does anything about it or not, whatever he does next, he will be an author. He does not know what kind of books he will write, or when he will do it, or how he will do it, but it will be so. *K'un* is patience, trust in the inevitable.

It's all up to him, of course. He will have to do it entirely by himself. That's the *Yang* of it, *Ch'ien.* To do it right, as a Superior Man, he will have to be righteously dedicated; it will be extremely difficult. But without a doubt, some future Michael Berman will have gotten it together, will have put all the pieces in the right place, will have organized his life for the sole purpose of writing… something… someday. It will be so.

He steps outside the trailer and assesses his surroundings. *La Resolana* is a fine place where he has found friends. His trailer is parked under a tree, one end of a Yucatan hammock wrapped around its trunk, the other end cinched to a high corner of his trailer. The air smells like flowers. Red *poinsettia* blossoms as big as dinner plates grow on vines climbing up the whitewashed walls. Profuse clumps of *bougainvillea* spill flowers down from the wall tops in purple, pink and orange cascades. Birds sing. Everything is good.

Karen seems stronger, her companionship less annoying. She will do whatever she pleases. As always, staying in the marriage will be her decision. He won't fight her either way. Patience.

Hannah is flourishing.

To hell with Dean, to hell with the past.

The future is beautiful.

PART FOUR

The Pool

Their trailer is parked in a coconut palm grove on the East coast of the Yucatan Peninsula on the Caribbean Sea. There are no other dwellings, permanent or portable, in sight. It's just the three of them, in their beloved trailer, at a spot where they can watch the porpoises hunting in the sun-warmed surf. Behind the palms is a forest where flocks of green parrots roost, leaving and returning every morning and evening. Pelican squadrons cruise above the rising waves, watchful for schools of fish.

Michael uses the fallen palm fronds that cover the ground as building material. In the two weeks since their arrival, using the tree trunks as supports, he's built little tables, a work bench, and a sunshade over an area above the hammock. The door of their trailer faces east, toward the sea.

Once or twice a day, they hear the thump of a coconut dropping somewhere nearby. On their first morning there, they had hired a couple of local men to harvest the nuts above their site. The men had shimmied up to the treetops and lopped off the biggest nuts with their machetes. Michael is not afraid of being struck by coconuts.

They are on a stretch of coastline called *Playa Del Carmen*. There's a little village where they buy their necessities only a mile away to the south, toward the Mayan ruins of *Tulum*. Forty miles farther up the coast to the north is a substantial town, Puerto Morelos. Beyond that. Another thirty miles farther away, developers are converting the wild, northeast shoulder of the Yucatan Peninsula into a resort they're calling Cancun. When the tide comes in at their beach, perfect wooden balls wash up, avocado seeds, kitchen waste from the hotels of Cozumel, a resort island they can see on the far horizon in the mornings.

He has been diving on the reef, exploring the warm underwater world of spiny lobsters, conchs, coral, and different kinds of pretty fish. He's found the perfect place a half mile walk down the beach. The coral heads are about a hundred yards out from shore at a narrow beach, accessible through shallow waters covering a white sand bottom. Some of the time, but not this morning, Karen and Hannah come with him and play in the shallows while he swims between coral heads. This morning, carrying his fins, mask and snorkel, he intends to swim out to a place where he thinks he's found the lair of an octopus.

When he gets there, no one is in sight, not even a boat between him and the horizon. He notices a faint path leading into the heavy brush. Curious, he follows the trail for a dozen claustrophobic paces, until he comes upon a *cenote*, a sink hole. These pits, often filled with fresh water from underground springs, are a common geological feature of the Yucatan Peninsula.

He sets his equipment on the ground and sits on the edge of the cenote, looking down into a limestone cup filled with still water. He sees the symbol of *Tao* in his mind's eye, and imagines that this pool is like the small black and white circles inside the identically opposite shapes of *Yin* and *Yang*.

He sees a crumbled stone path spiraling unevenly down to the surface. Swallows streak and swoop to catch insects attracted to fresh water, rattling the brittle greenery when they perch. What lives in this pool? Eels? Alligators? Pretty fish? How deep is it?

He makes his way around the edge of the cenote to the top of the broken path, and then step by step, downward, until he is only a foot or so above the surface. The rock on which he stands will be easy to climb onto when he decides to come out of the pool.

He puts on the fins and jumps in. The water is warm. He puts the mask on his face and the snorkel in his mouth. He begins by cruising near the surface, his arms pulling him forward, peering into the depths, the sun shining on his back. He takes a breath and dives.

Tiny gray fish with red speckled tails swim into view. The bottom is so deep that he can't tell how far down it is. The fish dart around him, delighted that a log, perhaps filled with yummy bugs, has dropped into their world. Then, he recognizes the species.

Really? Guppies! Yes, here at the end of a long, long road are fish like the ones he'd left behind in his aquarium. Guppies. The kind you can buy at any aquarium store, a dozen for a dollar. Guppies, the scorned common fish, the starter fish, the most ordinary of the ordinary. These are his old friends, the ones whose vitality and subtle beauty had struck him like a thunderbolt that time he'd taken the LSD, the acid trip when he'd realized that he'd been focused on all the wrong things. All this way. And here they are. And here he is. He explores all around the edge of the pool, and the only living things he sees are guppies.

He climbs out of the pool, takes off his mask, removes his rubber fins, and makes his way back through the brush onto the beach. He faces north and trudges back through the coarse sand, over fallen palms, beside the calm blue sea, walking slowly, to the campsite where his wife and daughter await his return.

"You're back soon," says Karen.

"Hi, Daddy," says Hannah. "Did you see the octopus?"

"No," he says. "Just some guppies in a pool. Can you believe it? Guppies."

"We used to have guppies, didn't we Daddy?"

"Yes we did. I wonder if they're still okay."

"I hope so," says Hannah.

He changes out of his swim suit and puts on his jeans, work shirt, and sandals. He has a full beard now, and his hair has grown over his ears.

He'd bought a machete and a sharpening stone at Puerto Morales. He keeps the blade keen and likes stripping the leaves and hacking the fronds to length to build his contrivances. He takes pleasure in making things, getting them right, at peace when weaving the palm leaves and tying the sturdy stems together with sisal twine. He used to enjoy writing his thesis, and fixing faucets at *Creekside Apartments*, and preparing lectures on the uses of evidence and testimony. It's all the same. It's all work, all useful effort.

Since their arrival on the Caribbean coast, it has dawned on him that he craves work. Whether constructing a table out of palm fronds, or getting students to learn, or fixing plumbing, he finds peace by doing the task at hand as well as possible, whatever it may be. It is the effort that satisfies him. He realizes that he needs to get back to any kind of useful work, to doing a job.

That's all. Someday, his job will be writing. It is his destiny. But not right away. The money will run out in a few months and he will have to earn a living. He's ready to end the journey.

No one knows how much he wants to write, not even Karen. Despite his fluency, the ease with which he finds the right words for any topic, Michael doesn't talk about himself. No one is interested. With regard to the writing, he doesn't want people to know his ambition lest they judge him if he doesn't succeed. He hasn't told Karen or anyone else about tossing the coins. What had happened was between him and the cosmos, personal, a secret. Anyway, they would think he's nuts.

He'd put the *I Ching* into a bin and hasn't looked at it since the morning he'd tossed the coins. But the experience had changed him, settled him. He has a new confidence, anticipating that any path he follows will ultimately bring him to his goal of a writing life, an artist's life. Until then, if he focuses on small tasks, doing what has to be done as well as he is able, if he tries to be a Superior Man, that will be satisfactory. He'd learned a lot by reading Lao Tzu's sayings and *The I Ching's* puzzles, but it's time to leave them behind and get back to work, any kind of work.

The guppies had closed the circle. His journey began with an appreciation for the miraculous beauty of the commonplace and the natural. And now the same creatures had been waiting to swim with him, after a year and five thousand miles of road, there they are. Wherever you go, there are miracles. So, go home.

Karen is sitting in a beach chair by the water's edge, wearing a big straw hat and her black tank suit, writing a letter. Hannah is a few feet away, working on the moat around a sand castle. He sits on the sand next to Karen, and says, "Do you know what I'm thinking?"

The End of the Road

Michael has gone off to swim on the reef.
Hannah is absorbed in drawing pictures of the birthday party they had organized for her in the campground near the Palenqué ruins. Fortunately, there had been another family with children there, who had been delighted by the idea of a birthday party in the jungle. They had stuffed a piñata with candy and enjoyed watching the kids flail away at it. Finally, after dozens of drawings of a black dog, Hannah is drawing pictures of something else - the piñata surrounded by blindfolded children with sticks.

When Hannah had crawled down from her bunk on the morning after Dean left, she had asked, "Why is Daddy over there?"

Karen had answered, "He just feels like it."

Michael had slept soundly the morning after his tantrum, through Hannah's breakfast of cereal and bananas, through cleanup, finally rousing himself conveniently when all the chores had been done. Then, and since, he's been a perfect, cheerful gentleman. And, since he's stopped wanting sex, the tension between them has abated.

Karen writes post cards to her parents and letters to her friends in Philadelphia, women whose weddings she had attended, young mothers like herself. During the weeks she'd been seeing Dean, she hadn't written to anyone. Since they had arrived on the Yucatan coast, she's written a few letters every day and drops them in the post box when she goes to the village.

Karen is writing to Renee Polanski, her friend who lives in Northeast Philadelphia.

"Dear Renee:

We found this amazing beach in Mexico. And we have a terrific campsite. We're right on the edge of the sea, all by ourselves. Michael goes swimming with his snorkel every day and is loving it. And we're all fine.

We will be home soon, probably in June. I have to get Hannah enrolled in kindergarten. Keep your eye out for good apartments. Michael is thinking about taking a teaching job in Philadelphia, so your neighborhood would be a good location. Look out for a two bedroom apartment. Nice, but not expensive. I will be so glad to get home.

I hope you and Eddie are still okay. Did he move back in?

It will be great to see you again.

Love,

Karen"

She folds the page and slides it into an envelope. She will have to buy postage in the village store tomorrow.

She doesn't know how to deal with this version of Michael. He has been pleasant, as if her affair with Dean had never happened. He had just moved on. Except for the sex, everything's the same as it has always been. Maybe better. He's always tinkering with something and he's been absorbed with building things out of palm fronds. He is great with Hannah, paying attention, tutoring, reading to her, loving her. As far as Karen can tell, their daughter has adjusted well to the new relationship between her parents.

And he's pleasant towards her, even attentive, as a friend would be. The only real difference between now and before is that they sleep in separate beds. He has finally put that Chinese puzzle book away. He carries a notebook around, sometimes sketching, sometimes writing. Once, she had asked to look at it.

"Please," he'd said. "I need a little privacy."

All in all, she'll take this version of Michael over any of the old ones.

But she doesn't know whether Michael will be coming back with her. He is not affectionate. It's as if he's taken a step back from her, given her more space. He has become like her, withdrawn, farther spreading the gap between them.

They had stayed at *La Resolana*, until their site lease expired on the last day of 1973. On New Years Day, they had hitched the trailer to the *Dodge* and headed south, toward the Mayan lands and the Caribbean coast.

She'd kept her eye on the gate during those final days in Oaxaca, but Dean did not return. Sometimes, on this isolated beach, an entire hour passes without her thinking about him. Dean had treated her as if she was beautiful, desirable, and irresistible. She had been all that mattered to a beautiful man and she had responded. Because Michael had been dissatisfied with their marriage, she had believed that she was unsatisfactory. Well guess what? She is absolutely okay as a woman! Oh yes. She will do fine on her own. She can get another man.

She sees Michael trudging along the beach, carrying his fins and snorkel.

Their relationship is so different without sex. She wants him back in her bed; doing it with him would reassure the marriage. But he doesn't want to. He doesn't try to touch her, keeps as much space between them as he can.

Karen might soon be in the same soup as Renee Polanski, who is up to her eyeballs in domestic troubles. She has two little kids and a problematic husband, a tense guy who hops from sales job to sales job. About a year ago, before the Bermans left for Mexico, Renee found out that

Eddie had been seeing another woman and kicked him out.

"You're back soon," she says.

Michael smiles. "I had a nice swim. I found this cenote just off the beach. I dove in it."

"Good for you," says Karen.

He goes inside to change. He looks good, she has to admit. He's leaner than he's ever been, deeply tanned, with smooth swimmer muscles. She even likes the beard. In some ways, he seems like a different man.

He comes out and goes back to his project, building chairs out of palm fronds. The first one fell apart and he's rebuilding it for the third or fourth time.

After awhile, Hannah tires of drawing and takes her pail and shovel to the water's edge.

Michael comes over and sits down next to her beach chair. He's seen guppies, and thinks that's some kind of big deal. But that's Michael, easily astonished. 'Oh look at that... oh look at this.'

He says, "Do you know what I'm thinking?"

"Not unless you tell me," she says.

"I'm thinking we should start heading home."

Hannah says, "I want to go home. I think it's a grand idea."

Karen allows some time to pass, waiting for Michael to drop the other shoe. Eventually, she says, "Okay... When?"

"Tomorrow would be fine with me. We can be back in Oaxaca in two days. I'll call ahead from Puerto Morelos and see if there's a site at *La Resolana*. We'll spend a few days there getting ready and just go straight north as fast as we can."

"Well good."

"I'll be sorry to leave here, though. We could stay here as long as we want. I don't think we'll ever find a nicer place."

"Make up your mind. Please."

"No, I really think it's time to go. Time to get on with it."

"You're sure?"

"Yes."

§ THE END §

ABOUT THE AUTHOR

Stanley Cutler writes historical mystery thrillers set in the mid-Twentieth Century, literary fiction, and essays on politics, communication, and human nature.

He draws on the experience of several careers, most recently as a planning consultant for Fortune 500 companies and government agencies. Earlier careers include computer programming, art salesman, real estate manager, and teacher at universities and public schools in the USA and abroad.

Other works include:

LOW LIGHT, 1st in the Rubin Family/ Dave Levitan Mystery Series

THE HOMEFRONT, a Dave Levitan Mystery

KILLER MATH, a Dave Levitan Mystery

TWO CONVENTIONS, essays on political and cultural evolution